UFO ™

SHADOW PLAY

UFO™

SHADOW PLAY

By James Swallow

ANDERSON
ENTERTAINMENT

Anderson Entertainment Limited
Third Floor, 86–90 Paul Street, London, EC2A 4NE

Shadow Play by James Swallow
Hardcover edition published
by Anderson Entertainment in 2024.

http://www.gerryanderson.com
ISBN: 978-1-914522-80-2

Editorial director: Jamie Anderson
Cover design: Marcus Stamps

Typeset by Rajendra Singh Bisht

TABLE OF CONTENTS

CHAPTER ONE

FAST AWAKE

Cold.

That was the first sensation that invaded his mind. An icy chill surrounded him, penetrating his flesh, aching deep into his bones. He was adrift, beneath the surface of a depthless, freezing ocean, all colour and form stolen from him. At the edges of his perception, there were impressions of dark motion. Shapes made of ink-black that wheeled and turned, patient and predatory.

He knew that if he turned to look down, if he dared to stare into the abyss below him, he would find something terrible. There was no name he could put to it, no way to give it an identity, but he *knew*, as sure as he lived.

A malignance lurked down there. A poison, capable of corroding the world.

Slowly, he began to rise, the cold still clinging. Threads of light – hazy and faint at first – seemed to search for him, probing the gloom. Sounds reached his ears, distorted and transformed until they were barely recognizable.

Were those human voices? The hiss and hum of machines? Or something else?

Something *alien*.

A glassy, brittle whirring brought up half-formed recollections of spinning crystal-metal orbs, ghost-lights glimpsed through the clawed limbs of dead trees, and things from other worlds.

And still he rose, the icy embrace of the ocean receding, the light growing brighter by the moment. The shifting shadows followed him up, gliding beyond his reach, dissolving every time he tried to focus on them, re-forming somewhere else.

Piece by broken piece, the world returned as the cold retreated into the void. He felt the soft, comforting firmness of a bed beneath his back, and the texture of cotton sheets on his skin. A flow of cool, dry oxygen caressed his face, emanating from a plastic mask that cupped his nose and mouth. Warmth crept in, and with what felt like a monumental effort, he managed to open his eyes.

His heart caught in his chest. High above him, a bright glass globe stared down, dominating everything – and for a terrifying second, he thought he saw it spinning, looming, coming down to take him.

But then the illusion vanished in a blink and he saw it for what it really was; just a dull light behind a hemisphere of plastic set in the ceiling, casting weak illumination over walls of grey concrete.

Attempting to turn his head brought a wave of pain that tightened around his skull, and forced an involuntary gasp from his lips.

From somewhere behind him, he heard the shuffle of movement. Then a woman's voice, prim and matter-of-fact.

"He's awake," she said. "Inform the chief medical officer."

"Welcome back, Commander." The doctor in the pale yellow smock leaned in close, flicking the bright nub of a penlight torch back and forth, observing the motion as his eyes followed it. "I must admit, you gave us quite a scare." He had a wolfish quality to him, with dark, shoulder-length hair that was starting to grey, and he spoke with a low, nasal accent.

The doctor's patient tried to respond, but all that came out was a desiccated, papery gasp. The soft tissues of his mouth were arid, and it was hard to form the words, as if he was out of practise with them.

"Here, drink this. Take your time." The doctor provided a squeeze-bottle of tepid water, and his patient accepted it gratefully.

"What...?" he managed, before his voice gave out again.

"What happened?" The doctor finished his question, slipping the penlight into a pocket before making a note on a pad. "We'll get to that soon enough, Commander. But I am afraid you have suffered a severe neurological shock, yes? And so, there are certain protocols that must be adhered to. A standard V-K series, just a few questions to... Ascertain your state of fitness."

He nodded, ignoring an ember of frustration, and gestured for the other man to carry on.

"First, can you tell me where we are?"

"Medical... Centre." He glanced around the small infirmary, confirming it for himself. "Level C... SHADO headquarters."

"What is SHADO?"

Unbidden, a tight half-smile, half-grimace crossed his face. *What indeed?* The endeavour that had consumed his life? That would be the most truthful answer.

He sipped more water, and spoke again, this time with surety. "The world's first... And last line of protection against non-terrestrial invaders. Supreme Headquarters Alien Defence Organization... A somewhat studied acronym, I'll grant you, but I think it's a fitting one."

The doctor gave a quiet murmur of amusement and made another notation. "Who am I?" He went on, without looking up.

"Doctor Douglas Jackson, CMO." The detail came to him easily, without hesitation; but with it there was more he left unsaid. 'Douglas Jackson' was a deliberately nondescript name, and he knew that it wasn't the one the doctor had been born with. Jackson's former identity was known only to a few, for reasons that neither of them would speak of. Like many of the men and women working for SHADO, he had a past that had been deliberately left behind after joining the organization.

Jackson handed over a few small colour images, photographs of faces taken from SHADO's personnel files. "Examine these and tell me the names of the people you see."

The first was an older man with thoughtful eyes in a smiling face. "Alec Freeman, second-in-command." The next, a younger guy with a cocky swagger that even the dull photo couldn't diminish. "Paul Foster, senior field commander." Then an elfin, auburn-haired woman with a gentle manner. "Gay Ellis, lunar operations commander." Each of them ranked among the organization's most seasoned, most capable operatives, and he knew them all. He took a breath and frowned, becoming impatient. "Doctor, is this really necessary?"

Jackson nodded at the photos, undeterred. "And that last one, please?"

The final picture showed a serious face framed by close-cut, ash-blond hair, a man bearing the weight of the world on his shoulders. The face was the one he saw in the mirror every day.

"Edward Straker," he said, his frown fading. "Commander-in-chief."

"And how long have you been in that role, Commander Straker?"

"*Forever.*" The bitter response slipped out before he could stop himself, and he sighed before correcting. "Over a decade now." He glanced up and saw that Jackson was, once more, taking notes. For a moment, the shadows at the edge of the room where the light didn't fall seemed to flicker, and he rubbed his eyes, banishing the mirage.

He shifted in the bed, drawing himself up, and again the tightness around his head drew in, making him hiss. "What next?" Straker didn't wait for a reply. "Are you going to bring out the ink blots and ask me to tell you about my mother?"

Jackson ignored the comment, seemingly satisfied that Straker's irritable tone was proof enough he was in a fit mental state. "Your pain will pass in due time. But I would caution you to take things slowly."

"What the hell happened to me?" Straker shot him a look. "I don't recall any details... Everything's fuzzy." He searched his recent memory, but it was like trying to hold on to a handful of sand, the recollection slipping through his fingers. The only thing that remained clear was the sense of that dream-like cold ocean and the dark poison somewhere far below. He dismissed the troubling thoughts with a shiver.

"Do you recognize this?" Jackson rose and moved across the room, to indicate a complex piece of medical equipment on a mobile rig. Straker noted what appeared to be a headset wired with sensors, connected to a small screen similar to those on an electro-encephalograph.

"Some kind of brain-wave monitor."

"More than that," said the doctor, tapping his chin in thought. "An experimental unit, something I have been developing with the help of the technical section. A testing device, Commander."

"Testing for what?"

A thin smile played over Jackson's lips. "Extra-sensory perception, no less. Paranormal ability. The human potentiality for psychic powers."

Something about the other man's words rang a distant bell for Straker. "You built an ESP detector."

"Precisely." Jackson laid a hand on the inert machine. "Our adversaries from space, the aliens in their u-foes... We know their technology is light years beyond that of humanity, but it is not their only vector of attack. Their mental capabilities are still a mystery to us... And that makes us vulnerable." He flicked a switch and the screen blinked on, showing the flat, steady line of a null wave form. "My ultimate intention is to use this detector to scan every member of SHADO's forces. Every operative, technician and officer, and determine which of them – if any – are ESP sensitive."

Straker considered that. With such information to hand, SHADO command could act accordingly, monitoring anyone who might be susceptible to telepathic influence, in much the same way they kept tabs on anyone who might be liable to coercion or blackmail. With a mission as important as theirs, operating in the deepest secrecy, it was vital to be sure there were no weak links that could be exploited by the enemy.

"The test process is somewhat... *challenging,*" noted Jackson. "The induction of acute physical and mental stress is, regrettably, a requirement."

Straker's hand involuntarily went to his temple. "You used it on me."

"Actually, you insisted that I do so," Jackson continued. "I believe your exact words were, *I won't have any of my people subjected to something I didn't go through myself.*"

"So what went wrong, doctor?" Straker was already assembling the missing pieces, putting it together. "And how come I don't remember it?"

Jackson looked away. "As I said, the unit is still in an experimental phase. There was a malfunction during the testing cycle, an overload. You suffered a neurological shock. You have been unconscious for three days. Some loss of short-term memory is to be expected."

Straker took that in, finding the gap in his recall where *something* should have been. He blinked, suddenly feeling weary, and again he saw that minute shimmer across the room's far shadows. "Is that all? Anything else I should be aware of?"

"There will be some physical fatigue. You may notice minor visual and aural after-effects, but none of this will be permanent. A few more days, Commander, perhaps a week of recovery, and you will be back to work."

"A week?" echoed Straker. "Oh, I don't think so, Doctor. You're telling me I've already lost seventy-two hours because of this? That's an eternity for SHADO! Do you have any idea what might have slipped past our defences in that time?"

Straker pushed up off the bed, making to get to his feet, but Jackson was already at his side, holding up a warning hand.

"Sir," he said firmly, his tone rising. "You may be the command authority on this base, but I am in charge of Medical Centre, and I am the one who determines who is and is not fit for duty." His eyes narrowed. "Please don't make me sedate you."

"You are *not* going to keep me in here, Jackson." Straker's tone turned icy, and the other man paled slightly.

"If you insist," said the doctor, after a moment. It was clear to Jackson that SHADO's commander would not take no for an answer. "But at the very least, as you have just awakened, you will allow me to conduct a few checks before releasing you."

Straker sat back, and gave a nod. "All right. But in the interim, have someone bring me the daily reports from Control. If I have to sit on my backside, the least I can do is make good use of the time."

"Very well." He could see that Jackson was displeased, but Straker had far more important things to consider.

The doctor took a blood draw and then left him alone, and once again Straker pushed himself to look into his memories, searching for some fragment of his missing time. His last firm recollection was of driving his car... *Wasn't it?* He remembered standing by a five-barred gate before some narrow, leafy country road, but he couldn't place the location. Had there been a sound? Like a breeze rushing through the trees... Or was it wind chimes?

Or something else?

As per Straker's orders, Lieutenant Ford dropped off copies of the daily logs and the commander immediately set to work, sifting through every detail of the last three days of operations.

Ford gave him an odd look – doubtless he wasn't used to seeing SHADO's most senior officer doing his job from an infirmary bed – and Straker dismissed him with a terse nod, losing himself in the austere numbers and facts arrayed on the print outs.

Like its namesake, SHADO operated in the places where the light did not reach, out of the public eye. Counter-intuitively, that often meant hiding in plain sight. The multi-level underground facility that was the organization's nerve centre operated on that principle. The cover for SHADO's primary base was a sprawling complex of film and television studios set in the English countryside. On the surface, it might have seemed an oddball choice as a location to conceal a clandestine military facility, but Harlington-Straker Studios had turned out to be the perfect fit. The movie business had its own requirements for security and obfuscation, and for the movement of equipment and personnel around the world at all times of the day and night.

If someone outside of the loop saw something, if they heard something that revealed too much of SHADO's real mission, well... they'd be told *it's just special effects, nothing unusual. You'll see it on the big screen next year...* And if that didn't work, there were other, more effective methods that could be deployed. It was unpleasantly easy to discredit a witness, given the right circumstances. Or, if the situation demanded it, to use invasive chemical means to wipe out their recently-formed memories.

Briefly, Straker entertained the possibility that something similar might have happened to him, but he dismissed the notion just as quickly. He knew the signs of the amnesia drug's effects, and he didn't see them in himself.

He returned to the logs, scanning the operations schedules. Like the proverbial spider at the centre of the web, SHADO Control had threads that reached around the planet, and beyond it into near-Earth space and out past the orbit of the Moon. They watched the skies, every minute of every day. Powerful computer systems, in advance of anything a single nation-state might be able to field, sifted and gathered intelligence, managing what would otherwise have been an impossible endeavour.

On the ground, fleets of armed Mobiles were deployed in key locations, ready to be activated at a moment's notice. SHADO's observers were secretly tied into military tracking stations and civilian radio telescopes in dozens of countries. A small flotilla of submarines, the Skydivers, were constantly on cruise out in the oceans, equipped to fast-launch a manned air-to-air fighter if a target breached the Earth's atmosphere. And in orbit, an autonomous intruder detector tirelessly monitored every possible angle of approach from the edges of the solar system. If anything did trip the SID's hyper-accurate sensors, then the call to action would go out to SHADO Control's lunar counterpart. At the Moonbase complex, a trio of Interceptor craft stood by to interdict any alien intruders.

It was a good system, crewed by the best people, using cutting edge hardware; but it wasn't perfect. There was only so much armour SHADO could put up around the world and still remain covert. The big lie – that mankind was alone in the universe – had to be maintained at all costs, unless the governments of the world were willing to entertain a wave of panic on a civilization-wide scale. And that meant there would always be gaps, places where the enemy could slip through the defences undetected.

It was this grim truth that kept Ed Straker up at night. It was what set him on this crusade, to defend his world against an alien foe he still knew so very little about.

And it drove him here and now, as he homed in on a specific line of data from an SID report less than ten hours old.

Straker stabbed at a button on an intercom next to his bedside. "Get Paul Foster down here right away," he demanded, and clicked off the call without waiting for an acknowledgement. As commander-in-chief, he was used to being obeyed.

There, on the page, in a string of numbers designating stellar co-ordinates, heading and velocity, a threat was lurking. By Straker's reckoning, the data could only indicate one thing. A UFO.

After all this time, he still had no firm idea of why they came. Unidentified flying objects, unknown aerial phenomena, foo fighters, sun-dogs... Whatever name they were given, they had been an observable mystery since the first formal reports began to trickle in during the 1930s, and a documented concern from the 1950s and into the present. Some even suggested that extra-terrestrial craft had visited Earth centuries, even millennia before that, but SHADO's focus was on *today*. Over the last ten or so years, u-foe sightings had taken on a more consistent and troubling tone, with uniform reports of alien craft, occupants and their hostile behaviour.

What had changed? There was no way to know, but SHADO had come into being because these alien intruders had gone from passive visitations, to acts of outright aggression. Abductions and killings, treating the people of Earth as little better than prey animals.

Perhaps these encounters were the precursor to an all-out invasion, or the desperate, predatory acts of a dying interstellar species. It didn't matter. SHADO's mission was to stop the aliens, whatever their intentions, no matter what insidious methods they used.

Straker looked up as Foster entered the room. The younger man didn't bother to hide the air of sullen displeasure around him, and halted at the foot of the bed with his arms folded over his chest. "You wanted to see me?"

"Yes. I admit, this isn't my usual office, but I'm afraid it'll have to suffice."

Foster smiled without warmth. "I'll make allowances."

The other man's curt manner gave Straker a moment's pause. Before being recruited into SHADO, Paul Foster had been a top-flight test pilot, so a streak of innate arrogance was practically threaded right through him. In point of fact, that characteristic had been one of the main reasons why Straker had brought Foster into the circle. But for now, he brushed it aside.

Straker held up the offending page of the logs. "I assume you've seen this sensor report from SID?"

"The possible sighting in sector two-five? Yes, I saw it. Computer says it's inconclusive."

Straker's lip curled. "The computers here do a lot, Paul, but they don't know how to simulate human instinct. And this report has mine buzzing."

"Human instinct," Foster echoed flatly. "The Space Intruder Detector logged a possible UFO sighting at the most extreme edge of its scanner range. So far out, that even a stripped-down Interceptor with additional propellant tanks couldn't get close enough to eyeball it. So we don't engage, not yet. The rulebook says, we observe and watch for a definite aspect change before committing to a course of action."

"Don't quote the technical operations manual to me. I wrote the damn thing." Straker's annoyance was starting to build. "We've seen this before. The aliens mounting sorties to probe our defences, looking for blind spots in our coverage. We don't have the luxury of ignoring them. We can't miss anything, we can't overlook anything. We have to be right every time. *They* only need to be lucky *once*."

"I'm well aware," Foster countered. "Moonbase concurred with the wait-and-see decision—"

"Did they?" Straker cut him off. "Well, as of now, I'm countermanding the directive."

"Why?"

"Because I run this place, and I get to do that," snapped Straker. "You're going up there on the next Lunar Module launch, and you're going to take direct operational control of the Interceptor force."

"To do what?" Foster eyed him. "Like I said, we can't go out after it, if there's even an *'it'* out there at all. SID's called false positives before, space debris and asteroids... There's no definite proof that what he picked up is an alien craft." He shook his head. "The whole thing could be a wild goose chase."

"Correction," insisted Straker, "There's no definite proof *yet*. That's what I'm sending you to get. And if it *is* a u-foe, you'll be right there to neutralize it. I want you on Moonbase until SID's sighting is confirmed, one way or another." He shot a look at the clock on the infirmary's wall. "If I were you, I'd get moving. The next carrier flight is in a couple of hours, so you'll need to hustle if you're going to make it."

But Foster didn't move. "Is this really the best use of my skills?"

"Those are my orders, Foster. Do you have a problem with executing them?"

The other man hesitated, as if he was about to challenge Straker again; but then his attitude shifted, turning formal and distant. "No," he said, "no problem." He turned and started to walk away.

"Oh, and one more thing, *Colonel*..." Straker looked down, back at the paperwork, putting hard emphasis on Foster's rank as he spoke. "Any time you want to add a 'sir' to the end of your sentences, you go right ahead."

Foster stiffened. "Excuse me, Commander. *Sir*."

When he was alone again in the room, Straker put down the logs and let out a long, low sigh.

What was that all about? He pinched the bridge of his nose, feeling the slow build of fatigue again.

Paul Foster was never a man to conceal his feelings or fail to call out what he disagreed with, but the tone of their conversation had almost edged into insubordination. Straker's gaze drifted to Jackson's prototype tester device in the corner of the room and he wondered, was Foster's reaction something to do with that?

Foster had always been a man of action, someone who believed in what he could see, hear and feel – and Straker had that in common with him. The whole concept of psychic abilities was a hard one to accept for men used to dealing with the unforgiving, practical realities of the world. It was numinous and vague at best, unbelievable at worst, the realm of mind-readers and spoon-benders rather than real science.

But then again, was it any more fantastic than the notion of intelligent alien life? There were too many incidences of strange phenomena in SHADO's past missions that could not be adequately explained.

Or perhaps Foster's ill-mood had a more prosaic explanation: he would have been the man in SHADO's responsibility seat for those three days while Straker was dead to the world. Most likely, Foster resented his commander's implication that he hadn't been doing the job by not acting on the SID sighting.

Well, let him, thought Straker, as he stifled a yawn. *A flight to Moonbase will give him plenty of time to think it over.*

He blinked, his eyelids getting heavy. Had the room grown darker, the light overhead turned dimmer? He couldn't be certain.

Straker stared down at the sheaf of reports, glowering at the lines of text. He was reading the same line over and over again, not really taking it in. His body was telling him what he didn't want to hear: *you need to rest, Ed.*

"Maybe," he said to the empty air. It was getting hard to keep his thoughts in order. He blinked, trying to shrug it off. "Maybe not."

The sensation was already coming upon him before Straker's mind caught up to it. The soft press of the bed and the sheets around him were cooling, the density of them increasing. He became aware of a creeping, sinister paralysis holding him down.

In astronaut training as a younger man, Straker had undergone centrifuge exercises to simulate the intense force of gravity experienced during a rocket launch. This sensation was the same, forcing him to gasp as he tried to drag a breath of air into his lungs. Suddenly, he couldn't move, he couldn't speak.

The colour slowly leached out of his vision, the dull hues of the medical room bleeding away into white and grey and black. And then there were the shadows at the edges of the light, creeping, growing, and spreading.

The slow nightmare he'd experienced before was forcing its way into the real world. The polar cold grew, and Straker felt as if the room was filling with brackish, inky seawater. It was there and yet it wasn't.

On some intellectual, clinical level, Straker knew he had to be hallucinating, he knew none of it could be real. But his mind and his body wouldn't accept that, the primitive animal part of his brain edging toward panic and the sickening chasm of claustrophobia.

No.

The denial echoed in his thoughts. He looked inward, grasping for the core of strength that had always been there. Too many times in his life, Ed Straker's iron will had been all that kept him alive. He struggled for it, pulling himself away from the cold and the darkness, sweat beading his forehead as he trembled and came back – step by determined step – from the brink.

Gradually, the cold and the pressure receded, and the thundering of Straker's pulse in his ears slowed to something approaching normal. He wasn't sure of how much time had passed – minutes? Hours? Fighting off a tremor in his hand, he reached for the squeeze-bottle of water and emptied the rest of it down his throat.

Straker sat there in the quiet, listening to the sound of his own panting breaths, straining to hear past that and catch the *other* noise he had heard. The whispers of voices, hard like crystal and too distant to be understood, out there in the ice-cold ocean he had dreamed of.

When he looked up, Jackson was standing in the doorway, watching him carefully. "Are you all right, Commander?" said the doctor, at length.

"Are we done here?" Straker countered with his own question, unwilling to supply the answer to Jackson's.

"It would seem so." Jackson had barely finished the sentence before Straker was swinging his legs out of the bed, rising to stand and get dressed. "I wish to go on record as stating your discharge is not advised, and is occurring against my medical advice—"

Straker spoke over his objection. "So noted," he said. "Get back to work on your ESP scanner, Doctor," he went on. "When you've got the thing perfected, we'll try this again."

"I am re-evaluating it," admitted Jackson. "The device may be inherently... unsafe."

"This is SHADO, Doctor," said Straker, as he slipped on a collarless shirt. "Nothing we do here is *safe*."

CHAPTER TWO

THE KNOWN UNKNOWN

Aside-effect of losing three days to a semi-comatose state was the hunger. Straker was ravenous, so after freshening up, he tore into a steak sandwich and a mug of strong, night-black coffee from the base commissary.

The mess hall was strangely quiet, and Straker couldn't shake off the peculiar sense of isolation in the long, echoing room. While he was practically alone, he had the creeping feeling of being watched. He glanced around. Aside from a couple of blue-uniformed security men taking a mandatory break, the place was his.

A hundred or so feet below the bustle of Harlington-Straker Studios, there were no windows to mark the passing of time, and only the hard, clinical illumination of artificial light. The base seemed to exist in a strange kind of *non-time*, where the passing of the hours was something that happened to the rest of the world.

It could be easy to lose yourself down here, he thought, *if you're not careful.*

As a quasi-military organization, primarily staffed by former soldiers, sailors and pilots, SHADO operated along lines that would be familiar to anyone who had ever served in uniform – and that included running on a rotating watch protocol broken up into six-hour shifts. That was fine with

Straker; his years of duty as an officer in the United States Air Force had ingrained in him an unconscious adherence to that kind of system. Straker glanced at the mess hall clock – it was mid-shift, hence the empty tables all around – but that didn't help to dispel the remoteness he felt.

"Burden of command and all that," Straker muttered, dismissing the thought as he drained the last of the coffee from his mug. Fortified and refreshed, he took the elevator up to Level A and the command centre that was the hub of SHADO's mission.

If the mess hall had been a study in silence, SHADO Control was the exact opposite.

The constant, low-level clatter of spinning magnetic tapes from the X-1 computer banks underscored everything in the space, as operators seated at their stations sent and received messages from the outposts of the organization. As a matter of habit, Straker's attention immediately went to the main display panel that dominated the far wall. On it, a series of glowing segments showed SHADO's current operational status and, most importantly, the alert condition.

Had a UFO been sighted within lunar approach range, that condition would have been vivid crimson, but for now it was a neutral green. Straker made a mental note to schedule a random tracking drill over the next few days to keep the operators on their toes. At any time, the Red Alert board could illuminate, and they had to be ready for it.

Lieutenant Thompson, one of the tracking team for the Northern Hemisphere Zone, was the first to see Straker enter the control room, and the commander noted the look of surprise on his face, quickly masked when the senior officer glanced his way. Thompson's reaction spread across the rest of the crew in a swift wave, the operators falling silent for an instant as they saw Straker among them. Some halted in mid-conversation before the moment caught up and they busied themselves with their various assignments.

Straker raised an eyebrow, but decided not to make a comment. *They're all surprised to see me back on duty,* he thought, rationalizing it away. *I wonder what's been said while I was gone.*

He tore off a length of fan-fold paper from the print out console as he passed, glancing at the most recent readouts from SID in orbit and the Earth-side electro-optical telescope clusters peering into the sky. So far, there had been no change regarding the sighting in sector two-five, and all other SHADO counter-invader assets – Mobiles, Skydivers and Interceptors – were showing ready status. Satisfied with what he saw, Straker strode purposefully across the room, the steel-plated door to his office automatically humming open as it sensed his approach.

The office wasn't empty.

In the far corner of the room, a man in a dark blue collarless jacket and matching trousers stood in front of the drink dispenser. He was helping himself to a generous measure of single malt whiskey.

Alec Freeman turned and saluted Straker with his glass. "Hope you don't mind. I worked up a thirst on the way over." In his late forties and easy-going with it, Straker's second-in-command gave a crooked smirk and took an appreciative sip of the scotch.

"Feel free, Alec." Straker returned a slight smile and went to his desk. "Aren't you supposed to be in California?" It was a surprise to see Freeman here, but it was a welcome one.

"What can I say? I got bored with all the pretty girls and sunshine."

"Oh, I doubt that." Of all the senior staff working for SHADO, the Englishman was the only one Straker would honestly consider to be a trusted friend. Their association went back a long way, before the creation of SHADO, before Straker's marriage, back to their common service in military intelligence.

"Actually, I'm here to deliver a status report to Henderson on the new US base. He wanted it presented to him in person, and as usual, he wouldn't take no for an answer."

Straker accepted that with a nod, taking a seat as Freeman did the same. While Straker was the de facto head of SHADO, there were still men he had to answer to, and James Henderson was at the top of that list. A former United States Air Force general and at one time Straker's commanding officer, to the outside world Henderson was now a civilian, the serving president of the International Astrophysical Commission. But in reality, he was the man who held the purse-strings for SHADO, and he was the bridge between the organization and the secret association of nation-states who funded their operations. It was an understatement to say Straker's relationship with Henderson was complex, and often adversarial. But they needed him, especially now that a secondary SHADO headquarters was in the process of being constructed on the other side of the world, beneath the Los Angeles branch of Harlington-Straker Studios.

"It's presenting its own unique problems," Freeman went on, anticipating Straker's unspoken question. "But we'll get there. Once the North American base is up and running, SHADO's global coverage will be virtually iron-clad."

"You don't need to convince me." Straker decided to take a slim cigarillo from a dispenser on his desk, lighting up before offering another one to Freeman. "It's not the manpower or the hardware I'm concerned about," he went on. "It's everything else. The things we can't quantify."

"*The known unknowns.*" Freeman gave a sage nod. "That's the trouble with this job. You and I, we came up during the Cold War. Our enemies might have been different to us, but at the end of the day they were still human. But all this?" He gestured at the walls around them. "It was created

26

to fight beings that are literally *alien*. Our usual rules don't apply to them."

Straker took a long draw from his cigar, and leaned forward to watch smoke curl from the tip. "When you give your report, make sure Henderson doesn't lose sight of that."

There was more weariness in his words than Straker would have liked, and Freeman caught it immediately. "How's business at this end?"

"Situation nominal," Straker deflected.

Freeman grunted softly. "Oh, I doubt that," he said, deliberately quoting Straker's earlier words back at him. "I ran into Foster on his way out. He wasn't in the best of moods."

"He'll get over it."

"He filled me in on what happened with Jackson's machine." Freeman sat back in his chair, fixing Straker with a measuring gaze. "You know, Ed, they put you behind that big desk there so you *don't* have to take unnecessary risks."

"It seemed like a good idea at the time." But the truth was, Straker had no memory of making the decision to subject himself to the punishing ESP experiment. He pushed that troubling thought to one side. "It's like you said, Alec. This isn't a conventional war we're fighting. We can't go at it using solely conventional means."

Freeman nodded grimly. "Yeah, we'll lose if we do. But you tell me, how do we defeat something we can't see or hear? Shooting down an invader ship is one thing, but fighting *powers of the mind*? I'd say it's the stuff of science fiction if that didn't sound like a bad joke. What do we really know about *them* and their abilities?"

Straker considered the question; it was one he had dwelt on many times. "They travel millions of miles, perhaps across light years, to harvest humans as if we were cattle. They take our healthy organs to replace their own decaying tissues... or even an entire living body as a vessel for another consciousness. In their natural state, they might not even be corporeal at all, at least in the way that we understand it."

"A life form that's nothing but mental energy." Freeman shook his head in near-disbelief. "Just a... a *shadow* of a living being? It's incredible to imagine."

Straker agreed. "We've seen plenty of evidence of the aliens using people who are psychically sensitive for their own ends. And we know they can duplicate the physical appearance of a living person, but not the mental component."

"Not yet," noted Freeman, glancing away. "Maybe that's what comes next."

"You and I are military men, Alec, but we're in a spy's war. And it's one-sided... We have no-one among them, but they have agents here. To succeed, the aliens have to utilize human catspaws."

"And sometimes, a *cat* catspaw," Freeman said with wry humour, recalling an incident where the invaders had used an animal as a kind of telepathic messenger.

"If they could muster a huge fleet of u-foes to attack Earth en masse, I believe they would have done it by now." Straker stared into the middle distance, thinking aloud. "Imagine the surge of panic that would erupt if they blasted their way across London or Paris, New York or Tokyo... but they choose not to. They don't want to go toe-to-toe with our world's military forces... Reasons? It could be they don't have the resources to commit to a full-scale interplanetary war. There's evidence of factionalism among them, some who might be unable or unwilling to fight. Or maybe this is just how they do things in their society." He sighed. "Whatever the motive, they've chosen stealth, infiltration and sabotage over open conflict."

"Are those tactics of patience or desperation?"

"*Both*. Us and them, we're all in the fight for survival." Straker felt an odd twist of tension in his chest as he said the words, as if they were coming from someone else. "Last man standing wins." He sighed, and ran a hand over his face.

"I'll ask you this just once," Freeman studied him, his usual bonhomie fading for a moment. "Not just as your second-in-command but also as your friend. Are you certain you're fit to be back on duty so soon?"

"I imagine you're not the only one thinking that," Straker admitted, throwing a nod toward the steel doors and the control centre beyond. "Sure, I'm used to having conversations stop when I walk in the room, and I know there might be concerns about me. But I wouldn't be sitting here if I didn't think I could hack it. I appreciate your concern, Alec. But I've handled worse, and I'll handle this."

"I've never known a man with as much drive as you," said Freeman, rising from his seat, dropping the stub of his spent cigar into an ashtray. "It's impressive, really. But just make sure it doesn't take you right off the edge of a cliff."

Straker's work grew to fill the hours that followed.

After Freeman's departure, he continued to scrutinise, then double- and triple-check every aspect of every log entry from the days he had missed. Helped along by more strong coffee, he filled the margins of the printouts with his additional notations. On the surface, the data seemed consistent with a low-incident profile, the distant phantom contact detected by SID notwithstanding. At any other time, Straker might have welcomed such a lull in alien activity, but here it struck him as *wrong*.

It was hard for him to articulate the cause behind his reasoning. There wasn't any one thing he could point to as an obvious anomaly. And perhaps that itself was the telling detail. Everything seemed too pat, too straight-forward and by the numbers. Straker couldn't dispel the nagging feeling that something more than time had gone missing, even if the logs said otherwise.

He crossed the office to the far wall, where a half-sphere alcove held a tiny representative model of the Earth-Moon system. It was a modern version of an ancient brass orrery. The simulacrum featured a blue-white globe in the centre, with the smaller lunar satellite turning slowly in its orbit around it. A light behind the glass hemisphere replicated the glow of the sun, allowing Straker to see a real-time representation of the Moon's relative position to the Earth, at any given moment.

Standing this close, he could hear the faint hum of the model's mechanism. The quiet clockwork of it, endlessly in orbit, around and around.

Going through the motions. Simulating something real.

The odd thought sent a shiver down his spine and Straker reacted, taking a step back. But he couldn't look away. His eyes were drawn to the black void behind the miniature spheres, and at once it seemed to become a depthless tunnel, reaching into a cold, abyssal ocean.

The room moved around him, even as his feet were rooted to the spot. Straker felt himself tipping forward, about to fall into the darkness.

"No." He screwed his eyes shut and bit out the word, forcing the sensation away with sheer physical effort. Straker took in a long, deep breath, and when he opened his eyes again, the momentary illusion had dissolved. Gone, as quickly as it had appeared.

Suddenly the office felt too small, too confined, the air stuffy and sour with traces of cigar smoke and stale coffee. He straightened, pulling himself together.

Maybe I did leave Medical too soon. Straker allowed the luxury of silently second-guessing himself. *But what's done is done. The mission won't wait for one man, that's the blunt truth of it.*

It was late now, deep in the middle of SHADO's night shift, and it would have been easy to call an end to things right there – but Straker couldn't bring himself to do so. Where would he go? Back to an empty home that he never really *lived* in? And for what? To go to bed, just to wake up in a few hours and come straight back here? His place was comfortable enough, but in all honesty, it was only somewhere to put himself when he needed rest.

SHADO was where Ed Straker *existed*. Everything else was superfluous. And after three days in a comatose state, he reasoned he'd had more than enough sleep for a good while.

I need to take a walk and clear my head.

Straker left the office, giving the control centre a cursory glance. The skeleton crew of night duty operators were busy at their panels, and he let them carry on without making his presence known.

He walked away, following the wide, low-ceiling corridors that edged the perimeter of the underground complex. Grey support spars of poured concrete stood out every few meters, marking off the distance. They cast lines of gloom where the overhead lights had dimmed into low-power, night-cycle mode. During the day shifts, Straker would have expected to see more staff on duty, even the odd electric buggy humming along the length of the passageway. But right now, he walked unaccompanied, the sound of his footsteps clicking dully off the floor.

Straker let his mind pick over the issue of the unresolved sighting, as he weighed the options before him. Foster would be on Moonbase in less than a day, and Straker wanted to have a plan in place by the time the other man touched down on the lunar surface.

Unbidden, that sense of isolation he had experienced in the mess hall rose up to the surface of his thoughts, and the skin on the back of his neck prickled. Alone in the quiet of the corridor, Straker could have been the only person in the entire complex. Just him, and the sound of his footsteps.

Up ahead, the passage ended in a T-junction, one path leading to the barracks for the base's enlisted contingent, the other looping back in the general direction of the control centre. Straker halted suddenly, on an impulse.

Off behind him, back the way he had come, the sound of an extra step echoed off the walls as if someone were following him, mimicking Straker's pace and gait, only to have been caught out.

Turning in place, he peered into the dimness further down the passage. Was somebody there? It was hard to be sure. During the night shift, only sectors of the facility in operation would be fully illuminated, the others kept dimmed as a power-saving measure. He took a wary step forward, retracing his path, listening for the echo, for the repeat of his footfall.

Straker froze – and there it was again, just a fraction of a second too late to be hidden. It could have been some trick of the ear, just the sound reverberating back at him. Or perhaps it was what Jackson had warned him about, some aural mirage left over from his ordeal with the ESP device. Whatever it was, Straker wasn't about to ignore it.

On the wall close at hand, there was a crisis pack beneath a service panel. Containing a fire extinguisher, a rudimentary medical kit and a flashlight, every room and corridor in the SHADO base had one, in case of an enemy attack or an emergency that left the underground facility without power. Straker pulled the flashlight and shone the narrow beam down the length of the corridor, aiming it right at the source of the footfall.

The light fell in a bright pool showing blank walls and vacant space. He cast it around, banishing the shadows, finding nothing.

Straker made a negative noise in the back of his throat, annoyed at giving in to a foolish compulsion. *This is SHADO headquarters,* he told himself, *not some damnable haunted house! What did you expect to see...?*

The footstep sounded again, closer this time, and unmistakable. Straker spun toward the noise, the white disc of the flashlight beam sweeping around toward the corridor junction.

A figure bolted away from the glow just as it fell upon them, and all Straker got was the briefest of impressions as it disappeared out of sight. Black from head to foot, fluid and fast, the shape was like the sketch of a man rendered in charcoal.

A shadow, cut free of whatever had cast it.

His jaw set, Straker dismissed the fanciful image supplied by his subconscious and broke into a sprint, dashing around the corner and into pursuit of the unknown figure. Up ahead, the corridor turned again at a right-angle, and the light from an overhead fluorescent tube captured a split-second of Straker's target in motion.

"Stop right there!" He shouted the command after the fleeing shade. "Identify yourself!"

His orders went ignored, and Straker ran on, turning again, finding himself at yet another junction point. Here, corridors went off in three different directions, and all of them were well-illuminated. Switching off the flashlight, he glanced around, looking for a doorway, a hatch, or some other means of egress the running figure might have used to evade him.

Straker heard more steps and looked up to find a pair of security guards coming his way. It was the same two men he'd seen back in the mess hall hours before, and he took a second, trying to pull up their names from his memory.

"Sergeant Bentley, sir," said the first of them, sensing Straker's hesitation. "We heard you call out... Is there a problem?"

Straker pointed down the corridor. "Did anybody come past you just now?"

"No one," Bentley replied, uncertain of the question. "As a matter of fact, you're the only person we've seen in the last hour."

"You've both been patrolling this level?"

Bentley's companion nodded. "That's right, sir. Standard sweep, as per protocol."

"Commander?" The sergeant studied him, frowning.

Straker gripped the flashlight tightly, the image of the running shadow fixed in his thoughts, aware that the next decision he made might reflect badly on him if it turned out be a trick of the light.

The odd, random sound. A flicker of movement where none existed. The momentary dissociation of a half-remembered dream. His tired mind filling in the gaps. These were all things that could be explained away by the lingering after-effects of his ordeal, or just plain ordinary exhaustion.

But it isn't that. I know it. I am certain.

"Listen to me carefully," said Straker, lowering his voice. "I'm ordering you to initiate an immediate base-wide lockdown. No-one in or out until I give the all-clear, do you understand?"

"A lockdown?" Bentley glanced around at the empty corridors. "But—"

"We have an intruder," Straker continued. Saying it out loud made the phantom become real, and with those words he had committed to the grim possibility that SHADO's airtight security had been breached. His grave statement brought both men up short. "Get it done quickly and quietly," he added.

The other guard shifted uncomfortably. "Is this a drill?"

"It seems not." Bentley gave the other guard a sharp look, then nodded back at Straker. "Understood, sir."

"And I'll need that," Straker added, pointing at the pistol in the holster on the sergeant's belt.

"Is… is it one of *them*?" The other security man paled as he ventured another question.

Straker took Bentley's sidearm and pulled back the slide, making certain there was a round in the chamber. "When I find out, I'll let you know."

The security men had come from one direction and Straker from another, which meant his errant shadow could only have gone down the third corridor leading from the junction.

With the flashlight held in his left hand, he put it up in front of him, crossing the pistol in his right over the wrist. The snub-nose silver barrel of the gun aimed down the path of the beam as Straker moved back onto the dimly-lit passageways of the base. He resolved that the next time he saw the intruder, if they failed to answer his challenge, a bullet would follow.

Can't take any chances, thought Straker. If it was one of his people, they would already know how big a risk they were taking, and if it was an infiltrator, they'd surrendered any chance of moderate treatment the moment they bypassed security. SHADO was a military base and that meant the use of lethal force was authorised within its walls.

It galled Straker that such an incursion was even possible. This wasn't the first time SHADO had been breached – despite the rigorous evaluation programme and secrecy vetting, some weak links occasionally slipped through. But those had all been insiders, men and women who were turned by external influences or coerced against their will. SHADO's fortifications had never been breached by an actual alien.

Is that what's happening here? A part of Straker felt as if he were leaping to the conclusion, but it was troubling how well the possibility seemed to fit. One way or another, he would know for sure.

Steady and sure-footed, Straker advanced, laying each step with care to make the minimum amount of noise. He strained to listen for sounds over the top of his own metered breaths, for the scrape of movement against the floor or the whispered shuffle of clothing.

Illumination fell at the far end of the corridor from around a right-angle turning and Straker clicked off the flashlight, letting his eyes adjust to the half-dark.

He heard a low, musical ping and recognized it immediately. Someone had called an elevator. There was a bank of them just around the corner, giving access to all five of the underground base's floors. Straker rocked off his heels and into a jog, and as he moved, he saw the light up ahead shift, heard the rattle of the lift car door opening. A shadow moved as an unseen figure entered the elevator as it arrived.

Straker was at a full-tilt run as he rounded the corner, just in time to see the lift door sliding home. He reached for it, desperate to catch a glimpse of who was inside, but it was too late. The mechanism whirred and the lift began to descend, level indicators flicking on and then off as it dropped away.

He slammed his palm against an intercom unit on the wall and barked out an order. "Control, this is Straker! I'm at elevator bank 2, there's a car in motion. Override the system, stop it dead!"

A few long seconds later, the harried voice of a junior operator came back to him. "*Sir, elevator control is not responding.*"

"Can you get video? Who's in there?"

"*Checking...*" He heard a faint sigh. "*Negative. Internal camera is out too.*"

"Of course it is." Straker bit down on a curse. "Can you at least tell me where they're going?"

"*Level E, sir,*" came the reply. "*Right down to the depths.*"

The operator's choice of words sent a cold prickle across Straker's skin, but he dismissed it, stabbing the call button for the other elevator. "Hear this. I'm going after them. I want every entrance and exit to Level E put under armed guard."

He considered for a moment what was down there – *technical systems, garage and maintenance spaces for the Mobiles, the main computer core, air and water processing...* The prickling of his flesh turned into a fully-fledged shiver. The enemy agent could be attempting to escape, possibly by using the underground tunnels that connected the garage to the surface. If that happened, he would never know where they had been or what they had done.

"Secure the blast barriers in the vehicle tunnels," he added. "We'll trap them."

"*Trap who, sir?*" But Straker didn't respond, marching away from the intercom, into the other elevator as it arrived.

The door rattled shut and he reached for the panel that would send it down to the base's lowest floor. His hand stopped, seemingly of its own accord, his finger hovering over the button labelled 'E'. Once more, Straker became acutely aware of his surroundings, of the smallness of the steel-walled lift car around him, the confinement of the metal box suspended there on a creaking cable.

His stomach flipped over, and he tasted a sour backwash of coffee in his mouth. He felt hyper-alert, every sound and detail abruptly rendered with vivid clarity.

Straker looked down at his outstretched hand and saw it was trembling. "What the hell is wrong with me...?" He muttered the question, unable to grasp where this strange paralysis had come from. *What am I afraid of?*

Ed Straker understood fear well enough. He'd flown combat jets into certain danger, he'd ridden atop prototype rockets filled with thousands of gallons of explosive fuel, and he'd walked in space with just a few inches of protective suit between his body and the killing vacuum. He *knew* fear, he'd looked it right in the eye.

But now some deep-seated terror was making him baulk. That horrible, blood-chilling dream that Straker had experienced during his blackout still, somehow, had its hooks in him.

The poison in the abyss down below. Waiting to swamp the world.

He shook off the bleak mental image with a physical effort, burning away the fear with something far stronger. *Anger.*

Whatever was down there, whatever kind of threat it represented, Straker would never allow himself to be intimidated by it. This was *his* base, it was *his* mission. *He* was the one in command.

Straker stabbed the button and the lift jolted into motion, dropping rapidly down past the other levels. He weighed the flashlight in one hand, then jammed it in a back pocket. The thing had good heft to it, and in a clinch it would work just as well as a makeshift cudgel.

He stepped back and to the right, away from the doors, bringing up the semi-automatic pistol into a two-handed grip. If someone was waiting for him, he'd be ready for them.

The lift car rattled and shuddered, and Straker shifted with the motion. His shoe came down in a small, inky puddle that had collected in the middle of the floor. It hadn't been there when he entered.

The lift moved again, this time more violently, and the lights flickered like strobes. Straker heard a grinding crunch beneath him and without warning the floor of the lift car was suddenly awash with an inches-deep swell of ice-cold water.

He gasped in shock. Each time the lights blinked off and then on, the level of the water seemed to surge higher – over his ankles, then to his knees, rising to his waist.

Straker pushed back, fighting off the undertow of panic trying to drag him down. He lost the pistol scrambling for the damp-slick, freezing-cold walls of the elevator as the water rose.

He knew there was a hatch in the ceiling of the car. If he could reach it, he could escape. Straker's fingertips scraped over the metal, but he couldn't find the seams or the latches. *It's not there,* his mind screamed, *I'm trapped in here!*

The lights went out for good and he was swamped by the darkness. He was going to drown in this steel box, his lungs filled with the metallic brine of seawater, the last breath of air choked out of him–

A flat ping sounded and the lift doors cranked open. Straker opened his eyes and saw the corridor vestibule for Level E out there before him. The gun he had commandeered from Sergeant Bentley lay on the floor where it had fallen. There was no floodwater, no murderous cold. The darkness he could have sworn was real had retreated as quickly as he had... *What?*

Imagined it?

Straker gathered up the weapon and cautiously stepped out. He was breathing hard, his heart hammering in his chest, and he fought to calm himself.

At first glance, Level E of SHADO headquarters looked much the same as Levels A through D. Identical concrete walls and angled supports, the same nondescript furniture, the same doors. Only the signage was different, with a colour-coding scheme in place to distinguish one tier from another.

The lowest level of the base also had the same night-shift low-light aura, and belatedly Straker realized that he should have ordered everything up to full 'daytime' brightness, the better to rob his target of any hiding places.

His pulse and breathing evened out. Straker threw a curious look back at the open lift. There was no pretending *that* hadn't just happened. A true hallucination, not just a stutter of sound or sight. He'd really felt the polar cold of that brackish water soaking through his clothing, the salt stinging his eyes and his face. How had it felt so *real*?

For a moment, he thought about going back into the lift, hitting the button for Level C to take him up to the Medical Centre. Straker was dogged and he considered himself a man of endurance, but he wasn't a fool. What he had experienced was unnatural.

I'm compromised. He imagined admitting that to Jackson. *I'm not fit for duty.*

What would happen then? He dreaded to think. *SHADO... The mission...* It was all he had. If that went away, then would Ed Straker even *exist* anymore?

But then he heard the footsteps again, and glimpsed the sinuous wraith that might have been a man, disappearing around the far end of the corridor.

Straker held the pistol tightly, his knuckles whitening around the grip, and he set off in pursuit.

At first, he'd thought he was chasing a fugitive, but slowly Straker began to suspect that the shadow-man wasn't really fleeing at all.

He's leading me. There was no other explanation for it. The intruder was taking too many risks, hesitating when they should have run, deliberately allowing Straker to catch sight of them just long enough to goad him into following.

"I'm not going to play this game," he muttered, aiming the pistol out in front of him.

He expected the intruder to head for the vehicle garage. Even with the access tunnels shut off, there were still armed Mobiles down there that might have been able to blast their way through the shutters. But the half-glimpsed figure doubled back, going deeper into the facility.

The further they went, the darker it became. Straker tried a wall panel to reactivate the overhead lighting but nothing worked. When he pulled the flashlight from his pocket, the beam was dim, as if the batteries were giving out. He scowled. He'd have to make do.

It wasn't just the gloom, either. The air became colder as he drew in, and there was a peculiar dampness about it. Straker reached out a hand and touched one of the walls. The concrete had a layer of dank moisture on the surface.

"I know you're here." The words bubbled up from him without conscious thought. "There's no way out. Show yourself."

Without warning, the scrape and crack of fast-moving footsteps burst into life, *behind him*. Straker whirled around, in time to see a black shape hurtling at him, on the attack, framed by faint light from back down the corridor.

He reacted on instinct, and fired. The pistol bucked twice in his hand, the hissing chug of the gunshots sounding around him. In that instant, brief flashes of muzzle flare lit up the dark and Straker saw only empty corridor. Bullets keened as they ricocheted off the concrete, hitting nothing.

But he felt the rush of wind as someone passed by, and cursed. *How could I have missed?*

He lurched forward, still gripping the gun firmly, and came upon the quadrant of the base where SHADO's computer centre was located. Weak, actinic light filtered out through a long observation window that looked in on the room beyond. Inside, rank upon rank of tall rectangular processing units chattered and hummed. Indicator lights blinked in sequence as the computers worked, tape spools constantly in motion spinning back and forth.

In a very real way, this section was the brain of SHADO. Not just the operating system that managed the flow of intelligence data and communications through the base, but also the institutional memory of the entire organization. Every last piece of data that SHADO had ever accumulated was in that room, from the latest set of lunar flight trajectories to the mission logs of every UFO encounter, from the most secure personal files of every SHADO operative, right down to matters as minor as office supply orders for Harlington-Straker Studios.

The shadow was in there, moving between the stacks, interfering with the machines. At once, a terrible understanding came over Straker. The intruder he'd been chasing, *they* were the poison, the creeping malignance that he had glimpsed in that strange dream.

And they were in the core of SHADO. Infecting it. *Corrupting it.*

"I'm already too late." Straker made for the door, the gun rising to the ready. He wouldn't be able to stop it, but perhaps he could prevent it from spreading –

"Ed. Do you hear me?"

The voice was firm and steady, close by. Straker stuttered to a halt and turned.

And things *changed.*

The gloomy dimness was gone, the corridor around him lit at normal levels. There, standing just a few feet away with his hands raised in a mollifying gesture, was Colonel Freeman.

"Ed?" he repeated. "It's me. Will you listen for a moment? Can you do that?"

"Alec? I thought you left..." Straker took a shaky breath, lost for an instant. Then he re-asserted control and straightened. "Doesn't matter, you're here, good." He jerked a thumb at the computer room. "I've got the intruder trapped in there, but we need to deal with them, right now! There's no telling what they've done to—"

"Commander," began Freeman, his tone firm but gentle. "There is no intruder. We've checked every level. The base hasn't been compromised."

"What? No, you're wrong, I saw him." Straker glared through the observation window, but it was like night and day. Inside the brightly-lit computer centre, the machines worked tirelessly, and beside them were two technicians frozen on the spot, staring back out at Straker and the pistol in his fist.

"Why don't you let me have that gun and we'll talk about this, all right?" Freeman extended his hand, palm out. "Just give it to me."

For the first time, Straker saw others further down the corridor – Sergeant Bentley and the second guard, both men armed with SHADO-issue sub-machineguns, and beside them, the watchful figure of Doctor Jackson.

"Give me the gun, Ed," repeated Freeman. He took a step closer, and Straker instinctively raised the pistol's muzzle to aim in his direction.

Bentley and the other guard instantly reacted, bringing their weapons high to cover him, fingers balancing on triggers.

"Please," said Straker's old friend. "Don't do anything we'll both regret."

The gun seemed to gain mass, weighing him down. "I saw it," insisted Straker. "I. Saw. It."

Then Freeman was right beside him, and slowly, calmly, he took the weapon from Straker's nerveless fingers.

CHAPTER THREE

THE SHADOW IN THE GLASS

Out of respect for his rank, the security men made the pretence of accompanying Straker rather than escorting him under armed guard. He knew things were not going to go well when, rather than return him to the Medical Centre, they took him to Level D, where SHADO's psychoanalytical laboratory was located.

Straker went without resisting. In truth, there was little else he could do, as he walked in stunned silence, trying to make sense of what had happened to him.

They left him in an interview room for the better part of an hour, and someone make the mistake of not closing the anteroom door across the way. In the quiet, Straker heard the faint murmur of voices in the corridor and caught half of a conversation.

Bentley, on guard outside, spoke furtively. "I dunno. Maybe the big man has cracked up under the strain of it all." The reply was lost, but then the sergeant spoke again. "And it's not like this is the first time, is it? I mean, being in charge of this place? It's enough to push anyone off the deep end."

Despite the bleakness of his situation, the man's comment brought a grunt of gallows humour from Straker. *Could be, he's right on the money.* He looked at his hands. *I did just wind up pointing a gun at my oldest friend.*

The door slid open all the way and a man entered. In his mid-forties with a mop of dark brown hair and wearing a canary-yellow tunic, he flashed Straker a wary smile. "Hello, Commander."

"Doctor Frazer." Straker glanced at the door as it sealed shut this time. "They handed me over to you, huh?"

Frazer's smile remained fixed. The doctor had a reputation among SHADO's staff as being something of an iron hand in a silk glove. He had a pleasant enough manner that masked an unforgiving, analytical mind. Useful when aimed toward problematic situations, the occasional double agent or unlucky civilian caught up in the organization's operations – but not so appealing when pointed right at you.

"How are you feeling?" Frazer added.

Straker's jaw hardened. "Frustrated," he admitted.

The doctor sat at the table between them. "That is to be expected. You've had a rather... uncommon experience." Frazer pushed a hidden button, causing a small console to rise out of a concealed section of the table. He gave it a cursory glance, then returned his attention to Straker. "Commander, I'd like you to tell me, in your own words and your own time, exactly why you initiated a base-wide lockdown, and why you came to the computer room brandishing a loaded firearm."

"It doesn't sound so smart when you put it like that," Straker offered, but the dry comment didn't gain him any more ground.

He took a breath and glanced around. Up in the corner of the room, a black plastic globe hid the lens and microphone of a closed-circuit camera, recording everything he said and did. There were dozens of other similar units installed throughout the underground base, but he guessed the live feed from this one was being scrutinized for every last detail. He imagined Freeman and Jackson in another room somewhere further down the corridor, discussing him and musing on the same variation of the question Sergeant Bentley had already asked.

Has Ed Straker finally cracked under the pressure?

"In your own time," repeated Frazer.

The doctor's manner chafed on him, and Straker met his gaze. "I believed there was a clear and present danger to this facility. An undetected intruder. I'm sure I don't need to tell you how serious that is."

"Absolutely not," agreed Frazer. "If that indeed was the situation."

"Are you saying that I imagined it?" Straker meant his reply to sound firm, as a challenge, but it came out wrong, more like an appeal.

"I'm saying I want to hear your interpretation of events." He made a *carry-on* gesture. "If you please."

Straker frowned, and he began from the moment he left his office, sticking to the basic facts of the matter. He went through things step by step, but omitted the moments in the medical room, the office, the elevator and the strange shift in his perceptions as he'd approached the computer centre. Despite the mounting evidence, he was still reluctant to admit out loud that his senses could be lying to him.

When he was done, Frazer gave a slight nod, then pivoted the desktop console toward Straker, revealing a small video screen. "I'm going to show you some security camera footage recorded earlier today."

On the tiny monitor, Straker saw a high angle on the interior of an elevator car, and there, squarely in the middle of the frame, he saw himself. An odd sense of dislocation came over him, as if the person on the screen wasn't Ed Straker at all. He watched as the man on the monitor stiffened, eyes widening in fright. The pistol he was carrying dropped from his hands and he stood rooted to the spot, visibly trembling.

Frazer watched him carefully. "Can you tell me what happened there, Commander? You seem to be in some distress."

"I really don't know," replied Straker. It was the truth, after a fashion, but not all of it.

"Very well." Frazer saw he wouldn't get any more than that for the moment, so he pressed another button, and the video playback jumped forward to a different time index and another location. "And here, can you tell me what you saw?"

The next footage was from the corridor near the computer centre. It wasn't dank and dim at all, but well-lit. Straker watched himself move across the frame and suddenly spin around to fire off two rounds at empty air.

"Colonel Freeman also said you spoke about an intruder." Frazer didn't look away. "Is that what were you shooting at? Can you describe them for me?"

"They were..." The half-formed sentence dissolved before Straker could finish it. What could he say here that wouldn't make him sound like he was paranoid and mentally disturbed? He couldn't fault Frazer for following this line of questioning, it was the job the doctor had been recruited to do.

Straker put himself in the other man's position. *If I were him, what would I say?* He didn't like the answer to that question.

For a brief moment, Straker thought about trying a ploy. He was still commander-in-chief, after all. All he needed to do was tell Frazer that the whole thing had been an exercise, cooked up to test the responses of his people. A thin excuse, certainly, but it would get him out of this room, give him time to get his head straight...

He stopped that train of thought dead in its tracks. *What am I thinking? I can't lie to my people.*

SHADO was built on a foundation of secrets, but equally it was important for everyone inside the organization to have mutual trust. Straker and his people had to certain that the men and women working beside them were solid and dependable. If they didn't have that, then SHADO would fall apart from the inside out and the aliens wouldn't need to fire a shot.

"I think, perhaps, I came back to work a little too soon." The admission wasn't an easy one to make. The razor-sharp headache he'd experienced on waking in Medical had returned, distant like a far-off thunderstorm but still ever-present. Straker rubbed his brow. He had pushed himself too hard, too fast.

"There's a phrase I've heard our astronaut crews use." Frazer sat back in his chair. "*Rapid unscheduled disassembly*. You've flown rockets and planes, Commander, I'm sure you've heard it."

Straker gave a nod. "It's a euphemism for the destructive break-up of an aerial vehicle. Typically deadpan fly-boy humour."

"Sometimes that happens, doesn't it? A jet exceeds its physical tolerances and just... comes apart. A rocket passes through incredible stresses during lift-off and some minor, hitherto unknown flaw triggers a catastrophic failure."

"I've lost friends to it." Straker could see where Frazer was going with this and he didn't want to follow.

"It's not just machines that suffer that kind of effect. It can happen to a mind, too. Even the strongest of us, under constant strain, day after day, can fall victim to it. All it takes is one thing, the wrong thing, to push us past the red line."

I am not losing my mind. Straker almost said the words out loud, but he knew that if he did, it would only make him sound desperate.

He felt like he was at war with himself. Part of him was ready to accept that perhaps something was wrong, that he needed help to get through it; but another part of Straker railed against that, convinced that however it had presented itself, whatever it was, he had seen something *real*.

Which was true?

He took a deep breath to centre his thoughts. "I think it would be best if I take a day... I'll need to head back up to Control, hand over temporary base authority..."

"There's no need for that," Frazer told him. "Colonel Freeman has already stepped in as interim commander-in-chief."

"Is that so?"

Frazer made a regretful face. "General Henderson felt it best, under the circumstances. You've been relieved of your duties, sir. Temporarily, of course. Until we get this all cleared up."

"Of course." Straker stiffened as the full import of that statement settled on him. "I need to speak to Alec, then."

"I'm afraid that won't be possible," said the doctor. "Colonel Freeman won't be available for quite some time. In the interim, we're going to run a few more checks." What Frazer said next made Straker's blood run cold. "We'll get you out from under this shadow soon enough, don't worry."

Jackson was the next to see him, entering via the anteroom. Once more, the door remained half-closed, and beyond Straker saw a glimpse of the corridor outside. The two security men had apparently been dismissed.

"How long do I have to remain here?" Straker dispensed with any niceties and got straight to it. "I'd like to leave, Doctor."

"You are not a prisoner, Commander." Jackson sat down across the table from him, busying himself with the desktop console. "If you would feel more comfortable, we can do this somewhere else. Your office? The lounge? Wherever you prefer."

"How about outside of SHADO headquarters?" He threw out the question, already knowing the answer.

"I am afraid not." Jackson's eyes flicked up to look at him, then back to the console. "That would not be a conducive assessment environment."

"And what assessment would that be?" Straker demanded.

Jackson showed him the screen. "I am going to display some images here, please tell me what you see."

"This again?" Straker folded his arms across his chest, weary with frustration. "Why not hook me up to a polygraph and be done with it?"

"Polygraphs are quite subjective, as I am sure you are aware. We will begin." Jackson pushed a button and a quick succession of five pictures flashed past – a cat, a dog, a house, a clock, a tree.

Reluctantly, Straker repeated them in order. The next batch were closer to home and came faster – a Mobile, the domes of Moonbase, an Interceptor, Sky One, and the Space Intruder Detector. Then Jackson tapped another key and this time Straker saw faces, flicking by at a rate so swift he could barely register them – his secretary Miss Ealand, Henderson, Foster, his old astro comrade Craig Collins, ending with a brunette woman with a blond-haired boy.

My wife... and my son? The screen held the last image for long seconds, and Straker had to make a near-physical effort to tear his gaze away. He focussed back on Jackson. "Whatever kind of response you're trying elicit from me, Doctor, I'd prefer you don't use my family in order to get it."

Jackson didn't acknowledge his comment. "Seeing them again, how does that make you feel?"

Hollow. The word pushed at his lips, but he stayed silent. When he searched inside himself, Straker found an empty space where their affection should have been. The sad truth of it was, that part of his life had gone away, lost forever.

With hindsight, it was apparent that his marriage to Mary had come at the worst possible time, just as the SHADO project was gaining momentum. Their relationship torn between duty and devotion, the cracks had started to show. Both of them had hoped the birth of their son would be enough to make them whole, make them a real family. But it had only delayed the inevitable.

And then his boy had died, and the guilt surrounding that cruel tragedy was like an open wound. Even now, Straker couldn't look at it, for fear that the despair he'd shuttered away might return and engulf him.

"This war," Straker offered, pacing his words. "It took them from me."

"And yet, you still fight on. You push everyone under your command as hard as you can, but no man more than yourself. Is it possible you may have finally reached a breaking point?"

Straker pulled himself back to the moment. "You want me to say that intruder was a hallucination?"

"Are you willing to accept it might be so?" Jackson studied him. "In the corridor and the elevator, you clearly experienced something disturbing, but you are reluctant to admit it. For want of a better term, perhaps it was an echo from the time you were unconscious?"

"I know what I saw," he insisted. "Where it might have come from, that I can't tell you..." Straker was going to say more, but the rest of his words were lost in the flicker of dark motion over Jackson's shoulder, out past the anteroom.

Ink-black, a shade in the shape of a man moved past the half-open door, dwelling for just a moment, as if pausing to take Straker's measure.

He closed his eyes, then opened them and looked again, hoping it would be gone. But the dark form was still there, and slowly it moved away, melting into nothing.

"Did you hear what I said, Commander?" Jackson was staring at him.

"What?"

"I told you that what the eye sees and the mind believes can be a misconception. You know this. How many u-foe sightings have been demystified and revealed as optical illusions or some other transient phenomena?"

"And how many do we know to be real?" Straker felt a surge of new impetus, and leaned forward in his chair, taking control of the conversation for the first time as a strange possibility occurred to him. "Doctor, what if... Your device, the ESP scanner, what if that malfunction *did something* to me?"

Jackson raised an eyebrow. "I do not follow your reasoning, Commander."

"You said it affects the mental state of whomever is hooked up to it, correct? But when it went wrong, when it knocked me out for three full days... Well, suppose when I came back from that, my perceptions had been, I don't know, *altered*."

"Intriguing." The doctor considered his words. "And what is the result?"

"I can see something you can't." Suddenly, it all made sense. The shadowy intruder, the strange flashes of sensation impinging on reality. Somehow, Straker's senses had shifted off beam, like a radio receiver tuning in to a different frequency. "I'm seeing what's being hidden from everyone else."

Always the scientist, Jackson didn't immediately dismiss the idea. He turned the notion over, examining it from every angle before he responded. "That is a fascinating theory, Commander. But it is also an extremely convenient, self-reinforcing delusion. It places you at the centre of things, it absolves you of any error or failure. It requires no material proof on your part, only that I believe you because you say it is so."

"I'm not an idiot, Jackson," retorted Straker. "I know how it sounds."

"Good!" The doctor smiled briefly. "That means you are still rational!" Jackson got to his feet and stepped away. "We are finished for the moment. I will have someone escort you to the visiting officer's quarters, you can get some rest there."

"I know the way. I don't need a chaperone."

"Commander's orders," Jackson replied. "You understand."

The base maintained a small dormitory section for junior ranks, simple single-bed spaces with a tiny washroom that any duty officer could use, if they were unable to get to outside accommodation during operations. More than once, Straker had thought about claiming one for himself on a permanent basis – but they were narrow and utilitarian, too much like a jail cell for his liking.

As Straker made his way along the corridor, his designated escort kept a respectful distance. Straker didn't try to engage the security man in conversation, there seemed little point. Instead, his thoughts turned inward.

He ruminated on Frazer's comment about Freeman taking command of the base. *That had been on Henderson's orders.* The ex-general wasted no time in activating the clause of the SHADO charter that let him stand down the acting commander's authority, if they were considered to be medically unfit. *He moved fast, all right,* Straker thought, wondering bitterly if his former mentor had even paused to reflect before replacing him.

Could this all be some gambit to get me cashiered? The question pushed itself forward before he could dismiss it. The deterioration of Straker and Henderson's relationship was a frequent source of friction between the two men, but he couldn't believe Henderson would be so calculating as to engineer a reason to be rid of him. *You're being paranoid, Ed,* Straker rebuked himself, *adding two and two and making five.*

"Here we are, sir." The security man indicated one of the doors, then stepped away to take up a post across the corridor. "I'll be just outside if you need anything."

"Right." The offer sounded genuine enough, but it only served to remind Straker that he was, for all intents and purposes, under guard.

As he reached for the button to open the sliding door, the low mutter of a voice reached him from the other end of the corridor. Straker glanced up and saw the flash of a pale yellow tunic. Frazer was there, half out of sight behind one of the angled support pillars, gesturing as he spoke to someone.

Straker took a half-step into the room, hesitating on the threshold. He had a compulsion to know who it was the doctor was talking to, and he couldn't look away. He couldn't hear the words, but the tone of the voices was serious. Frazer was shaking his head, as if making a grim prognosis, and he stepped back, disappearing from view.

Then Straker's blood ran cold when the other participant in the conversation ghosted into sight. Out of the light, all detail of face and form completely subsumed by darkness, the shadowed man followed Frazer out of view.

"Something the matter, sir?" The guard called out from behind him, noticing Straker's hesitation.

"No." Straker went into the room and let the door hiss shut.

Did I just see what I thought I saw? Frazer and the intruder, talking freely, probably talking about him. Was it another moment of his mind stitching together the real and the unreal, or was it exactly what he feared?

Have our enemies infiltrated this base? Is Frazer in on it? Or is it worse than that?

He sat heavily on the room's narrow bed and put his head in his hands. The distant ache in his temples was still there, it had never left. A hundred terrible possibilities, each one more chilling than the last, swirled in his thoughts.

What if I am right? What if something has been done to our computers, or our people? Straker recalled a random thought that had crossed his mind earlier, when he had contrasted SHADO's ill-lit lower levels to the corridors of a haunted house. *Maybe that's exactly what it is... But I'm the only one who can see the ghosts.*

It came to Straker that he would have to make a decision. He could either accept that he had suffered some kind of breakdown, that his judgement was impaired; or resist that conclusion and hold to what had always been his true compass. *His instinct.*

In the end, it wasn't even a choice.

Taylor, one of Frazer's medical orderlies, appeared soon after with a nondescript white tablet and a cup of water for Straker to take.

"From the doctor," she said. "To help you rest, sir."

"Thank you." Straker didn't really need to feign fatigue, but he put on a good show of being worn out, and popped the sedative in his mouth, following with the water. When the door hissed shut, he heard the faint thud of an electromagnetic lock closing him in.

Certain Taylor wouldn't be coming back, he spat the tablet back out, into the drain of the sink, washing away any trace of the drug from his mouth with more water. His senses would have to be sharp if he was going to act on his suspicions.

Casting around the sparsely-furnished room, Straker found what he would need. The upper handle of a sink tap unscrewed into three metal lugs, each no bigger than his thumb. The casing of a wireless telephone handset cracked under the weight of his foot, allowing Straker to remove the printed circuit board and the wires inside.

He used the board to lever open the door's control panel, exposing the electronic lock mechanism. He set to work, using his teeth to strip a length of insulation off the wires.

If it really was the enemy out there, pulling the strings, using the capabilities of SHADO against him, then they had made a grave miscalculation. Straker knew every inch of the underground base. He had been there when the first foundations were laid down, he knew every system and element intimately.

Working carefully, Straker found the correct points of contact and used the cannibalized wires from the handset to short-circuit the electro-lock. The magnetic bolt released and the door shifted open, no more than an inch.

He peered through the gap. The security guard was looking away, clearly unaware that anything was amiss. Straker closed his eyes for a moment, calling up a mental map of the level they were on. There was a service panel at the opposite end of the hallway, and it led to a maintenance catwalk that paralleled the base's elevator shafts. That panel was on an alarm circuit, but Straker knew where those contacts were located, and he could circumvent them just as he had the door lock. Once inside the duct, he'd be able to climb all the way up to Level A and the control centre, and hopefully find Alec Freeman.

Alec will listen to me, Straker decided. *Alec will believe me.*

He took a deep breath and prepared himself. He would only get one shot at this. If he failed, Straker would most likely end up in one of the nigh-impregnable holding cells deep in the bowels of the base.

He took one of the metal lugs from the tap between thumb and forefinger. Waiting for the right moment, when the guard looked away, Straker flicked the piece in the opposite direction. The metal ricocheted off the wall and the floor with a sharp click-clack, drawing the guard's immediate attention.

"Someone there?" The man moved away, his hand dropping to the butt of his pistol in its holster.

On a count of two, Straker slid open the door just enough to slip through the gap, then silently pulled it shut behind him. Pressing close to the wall, he stayed low, out of sight behind the support pillars as the guard investigated the distraction.

Waiting until the man was facing away, Straker pressed on, until he was at the service panel. It was difficult getting his fingertips around the seam, and for an instant he feared the guard would return and catch him in the act – but then the panel came open and he climbed through. The rest of the wires defeated the alert circuit, and Straker shifted his weight on to the narrow span of the catwalk.

It was dark all around. Cold, oily air came up from the lower levels of the elevator shaft, exhaled like breaths from the maw of an unseen monster. Faint red indicator lamps marked each tier of the base, extending up and down from where he crouched. With precious little ambient light, the dimensions of the shaft were difficult to determine, and it seemed to sink away into a bottomless abyss.

Straker's gut tightened, remembering the polar chill of freezing water washing over him, rising up from down there. He wondered if he would hear a distant splash if he dropped one of the metal lugs into the blackness.

Stay focused. He shook off the mental image, and took stock of his situation, finding a work ladder bolted to the inside wall of the shaft, at the other end of the catwalk. The climb wasn't far, but he would need to be sure-footed on the metal rungs. One slip, and he could fall to his death.

Up above, a motor growled and part of the darkness began to descend. One of the lift cars was coming down, thin blades of illumination from the lights inside tracing off the concrete as it moved. Straker held still as the lift drew level, and to his surprise, it stopped right next to him, the doors grinding open. The car shifted as someone stepped aboard it.

"Hold for a moment." Jackson's distinctive accent issued out of nowhere. "Are we certain this is the best way to proceed?"

There was an air grille in the lift car, and Straker leaned forward to peer through it. He saw Jackson standing inside, one hand on the elevator controls. Out in the corridor, where the light was cast, stood Frazer. And there beside him, still impossibly wreathed in darkness, was the shadow-figure that had dogged Straker's every waking moment since this nightmare began.

The dark figure spoke – but Straker heard nothing intelligible. The sound was peculiar, garbled, like a human voice slowed down so much that no meaning or intention could be determined from it. He concentrated, trying to pull out some kind of understanding, some sort of recognition of who or what this *thing* really was. But his gaze slipped off the shade's shape. He couldn't hold it in his vision, as if his mind was rebelling at the mere possibility of its existence.

What are you?

"I agree," Frazer was saying, concurring with the unheard reply. "I think we can handle the situation here. As long as we maintain containment around our subject, we're in control."

"Do not underestimate him," warned Jackson. "Right now, our subject, as you call him, is the most dangerous person on this base."

The shadow's distorted mutter broke in, drawing another nod from Frazer. "Termination is an option, if it comes to that," said the other doctor.

"After all this effort?" Jackson sneered. "That would be a waste, don't you think? I have already made my recommendation. We need to get everything we can from him, every last secret."

Listening to them discuss him as if he were nothing more than a lab rat sent a sickly rush through Straker's gut. But strangely, he found a new determination as well. Whatever deep-set, lingering doubts Straker had about his own state of mind, they faded away.

I was right. Damn me, but I was right from the start!

And this situation is far worse than I expected.

If Jackson and Frazer were compromised, that meant SHADO's entire medical department was suspect. Technically, the doctors could gain access to anyone or anywhere on the base, if they claimed it was because of a medical emergency.

It began to dawn on Straker that it might already be too late, that this gambit by the aliens was already too far along to stop.

He played out that grim possibility. If SHADO headquarters was under enemy influence, even partly so, where did that leave the rest of the organization? Isolated up on the Moon, the lunar base might still be secure, and the same could be said for the crews of the Skydiver submarines out on sea patrol. And then there was the new base on the other side of the world, still unfinished and yet to be fully staffed.

If I can get a message out, I could warn them.

But then, as if he was plucking the thought from Straker's mind, Jackson spoke again. "We should make certain the American facility is in step with us." Then he responded to what seemed like an order from the shadow-figure as it retreated into the gloom. "As you wish. It will take me a few hours to get there, of course, but there is an aircraft on standby I can utilize."

"Make contact when you touch down," said Frazer. "If there are any major issues in the meantime, we'll radio you en route."

"Understood." Jackson took his hand off the hold button and the lift doors closed. A moment later, the elevator car began to descend, and Straker watched it go.

Another difficult choice opened up before him. If Straker remained here, he would have to commit to reaching Alec Freeman, and hope that his old friend hadn't also been coerced by whatever power had affected Jackson and Frazer. If it didn't go his way, he'd have the entire base coming after him. The odds were poor on that option.

But if he could get out, get to somewhere beyond their influence, the story would play out differently. Jackson was now to be considered an enemy agent, and that meant Straker couldn't allow him to gain access to the new SHADO base. If both facilities fell to infiltrators, it would be the beginning of the end.

There is an aircraft on standby. Straker thought back on Jackson's words. The doctor could only have been referring to one thing.

As part of their clandestine mission, as well as Harlington-Straker Studios, a second element of SHADO operated in plain sight. Outwardly an aero freight corporation shipping bulk cargo, SHADair was the cover under which the organization moved operatives and hardware around the world. It would be simple enough for Jackson to co-opt a SHADair flight across the Atlantic.

Unless I stop him. Straker made his decision, and began the slow climb up the service ladder. *I know where he's going.*

CHAPTER FOUR

LOSS OF SIGNAL

The first faint hints of the dawn's glow gathered along the horizon, shading pink along the edges of the dark blue sky. Straker drove on with the headlights darkened, concentrating on the road and his quarry up ahead.

The early hour meant there was hardly any traffic on the highway, and *that* meant there were precious few other vehicles Straker could lose himself among. If the driver of the covered six-wheeler jeep up ahead caught sight of his tail, then this would all be over before it began.

Choosing caution over boldness, Straker eased off the accelerator and added to the gap between them. He was willing to take the risk. Jackson was in that jeep, and if Straker's instincts were on the money, then he already knew where it was headed.

Getting out of SHADO's underground base had been a challenge, but he managed it. Climbing to the top of the hidden facility's air ducts brought him out behind the façade of an elegant townhouse on the Harlington-Straker backlot, cleverly concealed from sight inside the hollow structure.

Straker ditched his jacket, stained soot-black during the ascent from the lower levels, and helped himself to a coat and a shapeless watch cap from a costume rack on Stage 6, where the last hours of a night-shoot were in progress.

It wasn't the best disguise, but it covered his shock of ash-blond hair and broke up his profile, enough that he could avoid notice by the studio's security guards. He made a mental note, that after this whole damnable situation was dealt with and things were back to normal, he'd have Paul Foster conduct a thorough review of base security, and close up all the loopholes Straker had exploited to get out unopposed.

The movie they were making here was a mid-budget contemporary drama, and that suited Straker perfectly. He knew they'd have the one other thing he needed – a vehicle.

It was a simple matter to select one of the production cars – a sleek, low-slung Experia coupe in dark blue – and take it off the grounds, flashing a stolen crew pass to get him through the exit gates.

Jackson was already on the road and a fair way gone by the time Straker was off the lot, but out in the countryside there were only a few paths that the SHADO transport could follow to its ultimate destination. It wasn't long before Straker ate up the distance and came upon the lone vehicle speeding through the pre-dawn.

Now, he took a turning off the main road and through an industrial estate as the journey's end grew closer. Low cloud overhead was staring to break up in advance of the sunrise, and Straker flicked a look at a clock on the car's dashboard.

Any time now, he thought; and less than a minute later, he heard the whine of jet engines in the distance. Off to his right, past the low, flat roofs of warehouses, a Cyranian Airlines jet climbed into the sky on plumes of bright thrust, the first departure of the new day from London's Heathrow Airport.

Early bird travellers would already be assembling in the terminals on the far side of the runways in the airport proper, ready for the civil flights lining up to follow that one. But Straker's interest was in this side of the sprawling complex, where Heathrow's air cargo hangars lined up alongside the secondary runway. He spotted a sign and the turn-off for SHADair's massive, curve-roofed building, but deliberately ignored it. Straker took the car down the next turning, to the offices of a logistics company whose staff had yet to arrive, and parked it out of sight from the road.

Staying concealed, he spotted the slower jeep make its way up to the SHADair security gate and halt for an ID check. He glimpsed the driver hand over a pass card, and then a moment later Jackson's distinctive wolfish profile appeared at a window, doing the same.

Entering through the front gate would get Straker caught instantly, but he didn't have the luxury of time needed to conceive of a clever plan. It had been over an hour since he escaped the sealed room back on the base, and there was no way to know if or when his guard might decide to check in on him. Add to that, the fact Jackson was here to catch a flight of his own, and it would depart on schedule no matter what.

Stealthily, Straker made his way down the fence-line, away from the SHADair hangars. While security was tight around that air cargo terminal, the same couldn't be said for the other tenants on this side of the airport. It was a problem that Straker himself had highlighted in review meetings more than once, but now he found himself grateful for it. In the next lot, there was a maintenance facility that serviced private helicopters for an air-taxi service, and Straker was able to slip past the men working on the rotorcraft and out on to the runway apron.

From there, it was a straight shot down the service road to the SHADair hangar. He just needed a way to blend in that wouldn't attract attention.

Hide in plain sight, he told himself. A small car was parked nearby, liveried in an unmissable bright yellow-and-black checkerboard design, topped with two flashing orange emergency lights and a glowing banner that read 'FOLLOW

ME'. Anyone would be able to see it coming a mile off, but that was the point – the 'follow me' cars were a common sight, used to lead aircraft around the airport's complicated taxiways, making sure there were no groundside snarl-ups that could slow arrivals and departures.

For the second time in as many hours, Straker stole a vehicle and set off toward his objective.

The sun was rising now, over the buildings and trees behind him, casting illumination down the runway and into the aircraft inside the SHADair hangar. A hulking metallic shape with high, angular wings and huge engines caught the light first. The Valkyrie cargo carrier was a giant craft, the biggest piece of machinery in the SHADO fleet. It could carry a strike element of Mobiles to any place in the world where there was a runway long enough to accommodate it, or even undergo conversion into an airborne command-and-control centre in extreme circumstances. It dwarfed the bullet-nose shapes of pair of Kingfisher tilt-rotors huddled beneath it, the smaller craft like two chicks taking cover below a mother bird's wings.

But it was the second plane, beside the cargo jet, that Straker was interested in. Sleek and arrow-sharp where the Valkyrie was broad and muscular, the Seagull supersonic transport sported twin tail-planes, a blade-like delta wing and a distinctive 'droop-snoot' nose cone. The Seagull was fast where the Valkyrie was capacious, and in the air, the only thing that could catch it was a Sky fighter.

Once aboard, the Seagull could get Jackson to SHADO's Californian outpost before the sun went down again, and he'd be free to initiate the next phase of whatever operation the aliens were planning.

A massed UFO landing? The obliteration of Moonbase? The blinding of SHADO? These were the doomsday scenarios, but each one was horribly plausible.

As expected, no-one gave the 'Follow Me' car a second look as it sped past the hangar's open doors. Straker slowed, scanning the interior, finding the blue jeep parked at the base of a loading ramp that extended from the Seagull's rear. He spotted Jackson boarding, swinging an attaché case at the end of his arm. Close by, a crimson fuel bowser was still in the process of topping off the jet's wing tanks.

I don't have long, he thought. *Once they're fully fuelled, that's it. Next stop, Los Angeles. Gotta find a way on board before then.*

He took the nimble runway car beyond the northerly end of the SHADair hangar and the second it was out of sight, he cranked the steering wheel around and skidded to a halt. Scrambling from the driver's seat, Straker pulled the watch cap down over his ears as far as it would go and set off at a quick pace.

He recalled something Freeman had told him about his experiences as an undercover intelligence agent in the field. *The key to bluffing your way into or out of a given situation is simple; just walk. If you run, people are going to notice. If you walk, if you look like you're supposed to be there, well... it's surprising how far that'll get you.*

"Time to put it to the test," Straker muttered, turning the corner back into the SHADair hangar. He aimed himself right at the Seagull's open cargo ramp, walking unhurriedly. The distance was sixty feet to the foot of the ramp, past the fuel bowser crew finishing up under the wing, past a loadmaster supervising the last pallets of gear being stowed on board, past a single security man whose attention was directed the wrong way.

Sixty feet. Then fifty.

Keep walking.

Forty feet away, thirty.

Only twenty feet to go—

"Hey! You!"

Straker knew the shout was directed at him. He slowed, his walk faltering, and finally he risked a look over his shoulder.

The Seagull's loadmaster, a skinny man with dark hair, was gesturing at a plastic hard-case container sitting on the ground. "Do me a favour, will you? Last minute addition. Get it in there, bay four?" The loadmaster looked harried, his attention in too many places at once, and Straker took advantage of it.

"Sure." He gathered up the case and hefted it on to his shoulder, so it would obscure his face, and carried on. *Couldn't have planned it better myself.* The case was his ticket on to the jet. No-one was going to look twice at another one of the ground crew stacking cargo.

He passed the security guard without incident, watching the fuel bowser's hoses detaching, and climbed the ramp as the red truck edged away. Above him, the wide exhaust nozzles of the Seagull's three jet engines hissed and ticked, the metal warming up as the aircraft prepared for take-off.

Straker did as he'd been ordered, securing the case on the deck with nylon tethers, all the time searching for a secluded spot where he could conceal himself. He would wait until the Seagull was airborne and levelled out at cruise altitude before he made his move.

He sensed movement behind him and heard someone speak. "Ah, cheers, mate!" Straker cursed silently but didn't turn around. The loadmaster had followed him on to the jet, bringing more containers of his own. He put down the stack just as another voice crackled over the aircraft's intercom.

"Flight deck; all ground crew are to deplane immediately. Departure is imminent."

"Right, come on then. Unless you want a free trip across the Atlantic, eh?" The loadmaster put a hand on Straker's shoulder.

He had hoped to get this done quietly, but now it seemed his brief moment of good luck was evaporating. Straker turned slightly, thinking through his next move. A light strobed around the cargo ramp, signifying it was about to start retracting.

The other man's eyes widened in a flash of recognition. "Here," he said, "aren't you–?"

Straker didn't let him finish the sentence. He whirled, bringing around a haymaker that caught the loadmaster completely by surprise, and slugged him in the jaw. The other man staggered back, bringing up his hands to defend himself as another announcement came over the intercom.

"Flight deck; securing doors, stand by for cross-check."

The ramp began to rise, the wide cargo hatches sliding closed, and the loadmaster threw a wild punch at Straker, more to force him back than to hit him. He lurched toward the rear doors, calling out in panic. If someone saw the man, heard him, the jet would be swarming with armed security guards in seconds.

Straker grabbed the loadmaster from behind and called on old reflexes he hadn't used in years. He snaked one arm around the man's neck and pulled back hard, choking off his air so he couldn't cry out, pressing against the carotid artery in his neck to slow the flow of blood to his brain.

The loadmaster panicked and fought back, but he didn't have Straker's tenacity. "Sorry about this," he told him. "Don't struggle."

At length, the other man gave a weak, low gasp, and Straker felt him go slack. He settled his unwitting victim on to the deck just as the aircraft started rolling, the triple engines in the compartment above building to a whining snarl as they came alive.

Acting quickly, Straker dragged the unconscious man into a corner of the bay and tied him up with more of the cargo straps. He'd be out of it for a good while, long enough for Straker to achieve what he had come here to do – find Jackson, get the facts, and put a stop to this madness.

The SHADair jet had take-off priority – an advantage to being part of a covert, United Nations-funded operation – and less than a minute after emerging from its hangar, the Seagull's canted nose lifted toward the sky and the airframe rose with it. The undercarriage left the runway and folded into the fuselage, and powering into the air, the jet shot away into the brightening morning like a loosed arrow.

Cleared for an unrestricted climb all the way up past thirty thousand feet, it was still only operating on less than fifty percent power. Once the Seagull made it to its designated altitude, the flight crew would pour on the thrust and take it to 'super cruise' mode at Mach one plus, faster than the speed of sound.

And in the belly of the beast, Straker waited for the tilt of the deck to ease back toward level, knowing that for better or worse, he had passed the point of no return.

"Flight deck; Seagull X-ray trans-oceanic clearance is confirmed. We'll be crossing the Irish Sea in about four minutes, then turning southwest across the North Atlantic. Estimated flight time to our destination is five hours and twenty-two minutes."

Doctor Jackson cocked his head to listen to the announcement, then returned to the contents of his briefcase. He had the jet's passenger cabin to himself, and had already used the automated facilities to brew a cup of strong, tarry coffee before finding a seat at an empty table along the mid-line. The roar of the Seagull's huge engines was cut down to a distant rumble in here, the compartment heavily sound-proofed so normal levels of conversation wouldn't be an inconvenience. To a casual observer, he might have seemed distracted, even bored. But in truth, Jackson was in a state of quiet anticipation.

Fate made sure that he didn't have long to wait.

He heard the hatch behind him hiss open, and Jackson looked up, a quizzical expression on his face. There wasn't supposed to be anyone else aboard the aircraft.

"Going on a trip, Doctor?" Straker entered the cabin, moving with care, pausing only to toss away the watch cap that had hidden his distinctive hair. "You left without saying goodbye."

"Commander." Jackson showed no outward shock at the other man's unexpected appearance. He put down the papers in his hands, taking pains to make no sudden motions. "Shouldn't you be resting?"

Straker took the seat across the table from the other man, one hand tucked out of sight, the other resting on the metal surface.

"If I may ask, are you carrying a weapon?" Jackson nodded toward the hand he couldn't see.

"I could be." Straker kept his expression in check. "I don't recommend testing the possibility. It might not go your way."

"For either of us. Firing a gun inside a pressurized cabin... that could have disastrous effects." Jackson smiled thinly, searching the other man's face for the tell-tale tics and micro-expressions that signalled a lie. But Straker had always been hard to read, a closed book even to those who knew him the best. "I have often wondered, Commander, do you play poker?"

"Occasionally," he replied. "Chess is more my speed."

Jackson leaned back in his seat, drawing his fingers into a steeple before him. "I will not waste time asking how you got aboard. The relevant question is, why?"

"I'm here to stop you," said Straker. "I'm here to carry out my duty."

"And what is that?"

"Protect the Earth. Protect SHADO. You know this, Jackson, you signed the same oath I did." He eyed the doctor coldly. "Tell me, when did they get to you? How was it done? Did you go willingly? How long have you been working for them?"

"You believe I am an agent of the aliens." Jackson frowned, beating back Straker's torrent of questions with one of his own. For a brief moment he lost his usual mask of clinical detachment. "How can you ask that of me? You, more than anyone, know what I gave up to be here. Do you really believe I could be a traitor to my own species?"

"After all I've seen in this job... after the last few days..." Straker gave a humourless grunt. "Frankly, I'm not sure what to believe anymore."

"I can help you with that." Jackson pulled a document from his attaché, along with a packet of Polish cigarettes, a lighter and a spectacles case. "Do you mind?" He pulled out a single cigarette and gestured with it. Jackson didn't wait for Straker's permission, and lit up, taking a short draw.

Beneath a *Top Secret* clearance code emblazoned in red ink, the file had the familiar circular sigil of SHADO on the cover. Straker couldn't stop his gaze being drawn to the image of a blacked-out figure casting his own shadowy outline on the ground. His skin prickled, haunted by the mental image of that odd humanoid shape he had stalked through darkened corridors.

"I recognise what motivates you," said Jackson, opening the file. "You seek to understand what is happening around you. But you are driven by your deep-seated compulsions, to the point that they blind you to reality."

Straker's jaw stiffened. "I'm in no mood for mind-games, Doctor."

"Then let us concentrate on the truth." Jackson tapped the pages in front of him, and suddenly Straker realised what the file contained.

"*Edward Straker,*" intoned Jackson, reading off the name at the top of the paper. "*Born 11th of June 1942, at Hope General Hospital in Boston, Massachusetts, United States of America. Rank: Commander. Current posting: Commander in Chief, SHADO operations.*" He looked up, meeting Straker's gaze. "There is quite a lot in here, you know. Your whole life is in these pages. School reports, college records, your application for the Air Force, astronaut induction, psychological profile... But these are just the dry facts, are they not? They are not the *truth* of the man."

"Is this the part where you tell me you know me better than I know myself?" Straker's lip curled. "I didn't track you down for a counselling session. But there *is* something I do want to know, more than anything else." He met Jackson's gaze and held it. "Tell me what they're planning. I want the details. Everything you know."

"You are mistaken." Jackson replied. "Everything I have done is because I am following the orders of my commanding officer."

"The man in the shadows? Him? Is that who you mean?"

Jackson gave a low chuckle. "We are always in the shadows, yes? It is in the name, after all."

Straker's skin tingled with a chill as he thought about the dark phantom he'd glimpsed down on the base's lower levels. "The computer centre... I know they've done something in there, corrupted it somehow. What's the endgame, Doctor?"

"That section is one of the most secure areas in SHADO, physically and electronically." Jackson shook his head. "It is virtually impregnable."

"Nothing is totally secure," Straker shot back. "There's always a way in. And they found it!"

Jackson glanced away, his tone becoming regretful. "You are correct, of course. No security apparatus can be total, there is always a weak link." He looked up again, eyeing Straker coldly. "And that weak link is the human element. Inevitably, even the strongest of us can break."

"I'll be sure to book an appointment if that ever happens," retorted Straker, his simmering anger building. The more the other man challenged him, the stronger Straker's defiance became.

"How would you know?" Jackson seized on his words, gesturing with the cigarette in his hand, the thin wisp of smoke from the tip drawing a line in the air between them. "A machine can be trusted to report its own malfunction, but not a man. And that is all you are, Commander, your sombre reputation notwithstanding. Even a man like you can lose his grip on reality."

Straker was silent for a lengthy moment before he spoke again. "I refuse to accept that."

"No?" Jackson leafed through the pages of the file on the table. "Consider the cumulative stress of every uncanny and paranormal event you have been subjected to. The frequent encounters with beings completely alien to humankind. The horrors of the extra-terrestrial bodies SHADO has recovered over the years…" He stabbed a finger at a line of text. "In the course of your duties, you have willingly exposed yourself to unknown forms of radiation and untested experimental drugs." He searched for a particular notation, nodding to himself as he found it. "By your own admission, you have experienced, and these are your exact words, *time-dilation phenomena* and *complete dream-state manipulation.*" Jackson's tone shifted, building to a damning conclusion. "Now answer me honestly… if you had a man under your command who had gone through such ordeals, and his current actions were questionable, would you not ask yourself, *is his judgement compromised?*"

"I'm not the problem here!" Straker almost shouted the retort back at him, his hands tightening into fists.

"How would you know?" Jackson repeated. "How many times can a man go through such things before his mind snaps?"

"I..." The building heat of Straker's anger switched to a sudden rush of cold horror, and he faltered.

What if he's right? The treasonous question snaked its way through his thoughts, undermining every bit of determination Straker had called upon since he had fled from the SHADO base. *What if it isn't the world that's gone wrong, but me?*

His gaze flicked away as something caught his eye in the far window across the cabin. Outside the fuselage of Seagull X-ray, bright blue sky and white clouds rolled by – but for an instant, Straker thought he saw something out there.

A shadow in the shape of a man? Or was it sunlight flashing off a glassy orb of spinning silver petals?

"Edward." Jackson rarely used Straker's first name, but he did so now, every sense of pronouncement fading from his manner as he reached for some sort of personal connection. "Please, my friend. See reason. Do not make this any worse than it already is."

Straker hesitated, and Jackson took the advantage. With a quick and fluid motion, the doctor took up the spectacles case and snapped it open, revealing the contents within – not a pair of glasses but a narrow auto-syringe loaded with a vial of yellow liquid. He was already guiding it to Straker's arm as the other man caught up, and resisted, grappling with him.

"What are you doing?"

Jackson didn't reply, and he and Straker stumbled away from the table, the injector caught between them as the two men fought to get control of it. The wiry doctor was stronger than he looked, refusing to give up the struggle, using everything he had to press the tiny needle home.

"You... never had a gun... after all," Jackson grunted.

Straker lost a step. He was worn out, pushed far beyond his limits, running on adrenaline and willpower. But he couldn't falter, not now, not after he had risked so much.

Jackson leaned, trying to shift the balance, and over-extended. His eyes widened as he realized his mistake, but it was too late to pull back. He lurched into Straker and the head of the auto-syringe stabbed the doctor in his chest, automatically injecting the full load of the drug into his bloodstream.

The other man gave a strangled gasp and fell away. Jackson's hands came up to grip his throat and he stared back at Straker with panic written across his features. His knees buckled and he went down in a heap on the deck, twitching in shock.

Warily, Straker dropped into a crouch and reached out to the other man, but Jackson's movements became disordered, his gasping breaths drawing out into a choked wheeze. The doctor fell silent, his eyes staring sightlessly up at nothing.

Straker touched a finger to Jackson's neck, searching for a pulse. He didn't find it.

"What the hell was in this?" He picked up the injector from where it had fallen, turning it over in hands. Despite suspecting that Jackson had switched sides, it was still a shock to believe that the other man had intended to kill him in cold blood.

Straker sagged back into the chair and stared at the dead man. It was all threatening to come apart around him, his plan to bust this whole thing wide open and drag it into the daylight. With Jackson gone, that meant the immediate threat was dealt with, but Straker still had only pieces of the complete plan. It was like fighting blindfolded against an enemy who could see every move coming. Straker could only react; he'd been one step behind throughout this mess, and he'd had enough of it.

The only thing he could be sure of, the only truth that hadn't shifted during everything that had happened, was that the enemy had done something down in the lower levels of SHADO headquarters. They'd managed to deter him before he could get in there and prevent it spreading, but that malignance hadn't gone away.

"I still have time to stop it," he said aloud, as a grim idea formed in the back of his mind.

Straker searched Jackson's body, finding the man's pass card, which he pocketed before rifling through the contents of the attaché case. He glared at the pages of his personnel file, looking at a photo of himself from a few years ago, back when SHADO had just begun operations.

He searched his own face for some inkling of what to do next, and once more, just as he had when watching himself on the video playback, Straker felt a peculiar sense of dislocation.

Did you ever think it would come to this? He silently asked the question of his other self. *Maybe I always knew it would.*

No alert sounded after Jackson fell, and nothing changed in Seagull X-ray's attitude, convincing Straker that his presence aboard the aircraft was still unknown.

He risked a look out through the cabin windows, but the view gave him no clue as to their whereabouts. Below was a featureless expanse of white clouds from horizon to horizon, and above, the sky shading gradually to dark azure. Soon the jet would accelerate to supersonic Mach Plus speeds, and Straker resolved to decide a course of action before then.

"Here we go," he breathed, and stepped through the forward hatch, into the service compartment adjoining the passenger cabin. A narrow gangway led up beyond a galley, through the neck of the jet to the flight deck, where Straker knew the crew would be at work. Seagull-class aircraft typically flew with a pilot, co-pilot, navigator and engineer, and there were no signs that any of them had left the cockpit since take-off.

Usually, Straker would have no problem convincing four SHADO operatives to follow his orders, but he had no idea if *these* men would obey him, and no way to know how they would react if they learned he'd just killed their only passenger in self-defence.

He couldn't take the chance the crew might be co-opted as well. *I need a convincer*, he thought, moving to a concealed locker beneath a hatch in the deck. A panel exposed the keypad for an electronic lock, and Straker used the ID code on Jackson's pass to open it. The hatch slid back, revealing a small rack of weapons.

Straker selected a semi-automatic pistol and two magazines of special frangible ammunition, recalling Jackson's earlier warning. Unlike conventional bullets, the frangible rounds were safe to fire inside the cabin, with enough power to injure an unarmoured person, but not to penetrate the jet's fuselage.

He weighed the gun in his hand, hoping that he wouldn't need to use it. Moving forward, Straker held the weapon behind his back, out of sight. He came to the hatch and listened, but the only sound he heard was the constant rumble of the Seagull's engines.

Straker took a breath and hit the control to open the cockpit hatch, steeling himself for whatever came next. He stepped through quickly, ready to confront the surprised aircrew before they could respond.

But Seagull X-ray's flight deck was empty.

Locking the cockpit hatch behind him, Straker slipped cautiously into the pilot's seat and ran an experienced eye over the supersonic jet's complex control panel. The dials and read-outs told the story: Seagull X-ray was cruising on automatic pilot, following a course out over the waters of the North Atlantic. Fuel state, altitude, heading, all were in the green. The aircraft was operating exactly as it should, just without any human involvement.

But that voice over the intercom... Straker recalled the crisp diction of the pilot's words earlier in the flight. *Where were they now? Had there ever been anyone else on the jet?*

In theory, it was possible to remotely control a jet as big as the Seagull – SHADO's technical section had looked into the technology as an emergency contingency – but to what end? Had this been some sort of elaborate trap to get Straker up here, alone and isolated?

He pushed that notion aside and let his old pilot's instincts come to the fore. There was an axiom that every flyer knew by heart, one to follow in the event of any airborne crisis. *Aviate. Navigate. Communicate.*

First, check that you can fly the aircraft. Straker reached up and disengaged the autopilot, and the jet shuddered slightly, answering his inputs as he applied gentle pressure on the control yoke. *So far, so good.*

Next, determine your position. He found an illuminated map display and dialled out the distance, until a glowing indicator blinked into life. *There we are.* He put the aircraft into a slow turn that would take it back around in a lazy circle.

Lastly, contact air traffic control and report your condition. Straker hesitated, wondering if that was the smartest move, but then pressed on regardless. He put on a discarded headset and took a breath.

"This is Seagull X-ray transmitting on guard frequency. Does anyone copy my transmission, over?" His only answer was a whisper of static. "SHADO Control from Seagull X-ray, do you read me, over?"

Nothing but dead air. A bleak scenario began to form in his mind. What if he had been allowed to escape from the base, what if the aliens had wanted that all along? Without Straker to interfere with their plans, they would be free to spread whatever malign influence they chose.

The darkness lurking in the depths could grow and build. He pictured it literally, like a fast-budding black mould spreading silently over the banks of SHADO's computers, strangling their mechanisms, corroding the wires and cables. Nothing would be spared.

He felt sick inside. "I've played right into their hands," Straker said to the air. "I've been following their script from the very start!" He shook his head. "No more. I'm going to end this."

Reaching for the throttle, he put more power into the Seagull's engines, angling the jet on to a heading that would quickly take it back over the British coast, and set it on a target, punching new destination co-ordinates into the map screen. The display re-centred itself on a patch of the Wessex countryside – the Harlington-Straker Studios complex.

"Attention, all SHADO stations on this frequency." He strapped himself into the seat and called out again over the silent radio. "This is Commander Straker. I am ordering a complete and total evacuation of SHADO headquarters and the above-ground cover facility." He glanced at the chronometer on the cockpit panel. It was still early morning, and that meant only a few of the civilian contingent who worked at Harlington-Straker Studios would be present. The evacuation order would trigger a fire alarm to get them clear, while the SHADO operatives would muster above ground in another location. "Initiate *immediately*," he went on. "Because in ten minutes time, there won't *be* a base to escape from."

An odd feeling of calm clarity settled on him, as Straker strapped in and committed to the only option that still remained. The SHADO headquarters was lost, he saw that now. But the canker the aliens had implanted down there was still alive, still capable of malevolence. He had to destroy it, even if that meant losing the facility as well.

And his only weapon was this aircraft.

I can do it, he reasoned. He would take the jet down as fast as he dared, aiming Seagull X-ray like a guided missile straight at the heart of the studio sprawl. It would act like a bunker-buster bomb, blasting through into the hidden base, consuming everything in a storm of octane fire.

SHADO would explain it away as some terrible freak accident – after all, cover-ups were part of the job – but the threat would be neutralized.

"Ed!" Alec Freeman's voice crackled over the radio. *"That's you up there? We're reading you on a collision course... for god's sake, man, what are you thinking?"*

"Get out of the base, Alec," he told him. "While you still can. I have to do this. It's the only way to be sure."

"We'll lose everything we've built here... and you'll die!"

"That's not my first plan. I guess we'll see if the Seagull's ejection system is up to the job. If not..." He trailed off.

"Ed, there is no enemy here, can't you see that? I can't let you do this."

"You can't stop me."

"You're wrong about that." Freeman gave a sorrowful sigh. Then his tone shifted, becoming business-like as he addressed someone else. *"Skydiver, say launch status, over?"*

"Sky One is airborne." A familiar voice gave a clipped reply over the open channel. *"On heading two-zero-zero, time to intercept, thirty seconds."*

"Foster?" It seemed that Straker's orders to send the colonel to Moonbase had been disregarded after all.

"Sky One, your target is Seagull X-ray," said Freeman. "Shoot it down."

"Target confirmed. Missiles armed. Moving to engage."

Straker shot a look out of the cockpit canopy, in time to spot a dark green dart emerge from the thinning cloud bank below, rising at a high angle of attack. The Sky fighter was turning to bear. He had only moments before Foster opened fire.

Ahead of the Seagull's nose, the ground was widening to fill the view through the windows. Straker pressed the flight yoke all the way forward and the jet screamed as it powered into a headlong crash-dive.

After double-checking his straps, Straker's hand dropped to a bright orange handle controlling the ejector seat and he pulled hard. The mechanism jolted and locked, refusing to engage. Straker pulled again, and still it would not activate.

"That's the choice made for me, then," he muttered, just as Foster called out over the radio.

"Sky One firing... missiles away!"

Straker wanted to close his eyes, but he couldn't bring himself to do it. He would see this to its end.

Then the view outside the canopy flickered and slowed, turning a brilliant white; and everything else was smothered by a sudden silence.

From somewhere far above him, he heard a distorted voice say: "This has gone far enough."

CHAPTER FIVE

THE MAN WITH MY FACE

At the end, he had expected death. A millisecond of brilliant fire, an all-consuming agony and then nothingness.

When it came right down to it, Straker wasn't much of a believer in abstract concepts like an afterlife, or that kind of thing. It was all too mystical, too hard to grab hold of. He had lived his whole life in the now, firm in the belief that he would only get one shot at existence before it all went away.

He hadn't expected this, the world around him cranking to a sudden halt, the fire and pain vanishing before they even came to pass.

Slowly, he took his hands off the Seagull's flight yoke, pulled the radio headset from his ear, and listened.

Silence.

The shrieking chorus of jet's massive engines was gone, without an echo to mark it. The anguished, intense voices of Freeman and Foster over the radio had been stilled.

Straker unstrapped from the pilot's chair, and pushed forward to peer out of the canopy. Where before there had been a vista of sky, now there was only a featureless white void bereft of depth or scale.

He took the gun he'd secured from the weapons locker and made his way off the flight deck. The deck creaked as he moved, and somewhere outside Straker heard a sound like footfalls.

The exterior access door in the side of the Seagull's fuselage was hanging open. It had been sealed shut before when the jet was thousands of feet up – *if it ever had been?* – but now it was mute invitation for Straker to follow this mystery to whatever conclusion awaited him.

He stepped out, making his way down a metal staircase. A high ceiling loomed overhead, heavy with shadows, and Straker made out skeletal catwalks up there, along with dozens of dangling cables hanging out of the dark, some ending in the drums of spotlights. The place was almost as big and as open as the SHADair hangar at Heathrow, but it had a stuffy and enclosed quality to it where the walls were lined with thick, sound-deadening material.

He knew this place: it was Soundstage #2, the biggest interior space on the Harlington-Straker lot, usually dedicated to only the largest of the studio's big budget productions. Glancing back toward the Seagull, instead of seeing the sleek white fuselage, his gaze fell on a rough construction of wood up on a hydraulic suspension rig. A set within the stage, the false reality of an aircraft without wings. Where the conical nosecone and cockpit should have been, he saw the blank white form of a back-projection screen wrapped around the canopy windows.

He hissed as a jolt of pain crackled around the inside of his skull, as if seeing the evidence of his own eyes had set it off.

"This... is not possible." Straker stepped down from the staircase, casting around. "I was there. I was aboard that aircraft, it was real!"

"A trick of the light." That strange, distorted voice he'd heard before came at him from out of the darkness, warping and changing with each uttered word. "A false reality, rendered at twenty-four frames per second."

"Who are you?" Straker turned in the direction of the sound. "Show yourself."

"But this is a film studio, isn't it?" Buoyed on footsteps, a dark shape broke away from the gloom before him. A figure, made out of shadows, coming closer. "*Illusion*. That's what they manufacture here, day in and day out."

Straker gripped his pistol tightly, expecting at last to see the aspect of his perpetual enemy revealed – a silver helmet framing an alien's pallid green complexion, a humanoid form sheathed in fabric the colour of blood. But what approached was a man, the blackness seeming to slough off him as he moved, revealing... *who?*

Straker found himself looking into hard, searching eyes framed by ash-blond hair, into the face of a man who did not flinch, did not turn away.

It was the face from the file Jackson had used to taunt him. The same one he saw in the mirror.

"What the devil are you?" He brought up the gun, and the Other Straker halted.

"I imagine that's not the only question you have," came the reply, as the distortion in the voice finally faded away.

"I was on board Seagull X-ray. I escaped from SHADO, I drove to the airport, got on to the plane..." Straker shook his head. "It would be impossible to fake all of that!"

"I'll admit, I was sceptical that it could be done," said the doppelganger. "But Doctor Jackson convinced me it was possible. A combination of psychoactive drugs covertly administered, some hypnotic suggestion, and false scenes like this..." He gestured toward the set of the jet aircraft. "Most people don't realize that the mind is so pliable. It can be quite a shock to find out how easy it is to alter someone's perceptions."

"Jackson." Straker hung up on the man's name. "I... there was a struggle, he had an injector..."

The other man said nothing, indicating something off behind the suspended set with a jerk of his chin. Turning, Straker saw two figures walking away, briefly outlined by bright daylight as they passed out of the soundstage through a side door. One was the loadmaster he had fought with on the cargo deck, and the other was Jackson, alive and well. The doctor threw him a wry salute and then he was gone.

"Don't worry. You haven't killed anyone," said the Other Straker.

"Not yet." He kept his weapon aimed at his double, finding some steel in his response. "But the day is young."

"Interesting." That brought a wry smirk. "I never thought I'd be capable of killing myself. Yet here you are, threatening to do it for a second time today." The man came another step closer. "You really would have followed through, wouldn't you? You were ready to ride that jet the whole way down, and go out in a blaze of glory."

"If you're supposed to be me, then you already know the answer." Straker gestured at his face. "All this you have... it's too good to be a mask. But the aliens have made physical copies of us before, haven't they?"

The other man nodded. "Yes, that business with the dome beneath the sea. They got almost every detail correct, at least on a surface level. But they couldn't crack the voices. Almost like they don't really understand how humans work, like they can simulate the image but not the content. Mimicry, not duplication."

The incident in question had been a bold enemy gambit to bypass SHADO's defences. The invaders had created physical replicas of everyone in the base's command centre and the control room itself. In a kind of grotesque pantomime, they used edited recordings of radio communications to stand down the Interceptor and Skydiver fleets. If not for

Foster and Straker leading a mission to the alien outpost on the Atlantic sea floor, it might have worked.

But those *things* in that dome, those ersatz 'reflections' were more like automata, flesh and blood but only capable of limited, aggressive actions. When the base had been destroyed, nothing remained of them, and SHADO's commander quietly hoped that the aliens wouldn't seek to improve on their creations.

Looking into the eyes of his twin, Straker saw now that hope had been in vain. "How many are there? How many doubles have infiltrated SHADO?"

"Just the one," said the other man. "They decided to start at the top."

"Makes sense," he replied. "But from where I'm standing, it doesn't look like it's working out."

"On that, we can agree." The Other Straker gave a rueful nod.

Out beyond the walls of the soundstage, metal clattered against metal, and Straker's mind caught up to a troubling possibility. *He's stalling for time. Waiting for Jackson to come back with reinforcements.*

"Move!" He jerked the pistol toward the far end of the stage, where a knife of daylight crept in through a gap in the towering main doors. "That way!"

"Where are we going?" said the other man. He began to walk, holding out his hands to his sides to show he was no threat. "Do you even have a plan of action at this point? Or are you just reacting? Trust me, I know that look."

"I'm adapting and improvising," he shot back. "Keep walking. And don't try anything."

"I wouldn't dream of it."

They emerged into the brightness of day, and Straker was careful, knowing that it was the perfect moment to attack, while his eyes adjusted from the gloomy interior of the soundstage.

But his counterpart did nothing, continuing to lead the way down the narrow service street between the steel-walled main stage and its smaller brick-built neighbours.

If anyone else was close by, they were keeping out of sight. At Straker's direction, they started toward the main office block overlooking the studio complex, passing the fabrication shops where scenery flats were built and painted.

Movement at the edge of his vision caught Straker's eye and he threw a look to one side, where the cluttered interior of the prop store was visible. He saw an eclectic mix of objects – a Regency-era dining table and chairs, a giant white hand resting on a wooden base, a red telephone call box and other ephemera – but no lurking figures waiting to ambush them. The motion was only the breeze disturbing a drooping flag that hung on a wall.

"If we wanted you eliminated," said the other man, noting his attention, "there would be a sniper with you in their crosshairs right now."

"Risky play," he replied. "Who would you trust not to accidentally put a bullet in the wrong head?"

"That's a fair point."

They passed through the studio's standing sets that stood ghost-town empty, along fake boulevards that resembled some nameless replica of a European city. From one angle, the buildings appeared complete and whole, and the roads led away to a vanishing point. But if one looked closer, it was clear they were all false frontages, and the streets ended in forced-perspective backdrops that went nowhere. The irony of it wasn't lost on Straker, as he marched his double onward.

He thought again about the comment the Other Straker had made. "Why am I here? *You're* here," he said to the back of the figure in front of him. "It's a liability having two of us in the same place. So why keep me around?" The pain in his head had returned with a vengeance now, dogging him with every step he took.

Predictably, the reply he got was oblique. "Why do you think?"

Why indeed? Straker answered his own question aloud. "So the aliens have gotten better at this, but they still can't get us right, not completely. They can copy a face, a body, and now even the voice...."

"And more," said the other man. "Jackson has a theory. They're telepathic beings, on some level, that's a confirmed fact. So perhaps, under the right conditions, they can read the surface details of human memory and personality. Take that, combine it with the intelligence they already have on the senior staff of SHADO, along with anything else they can glean about us. Together, it might be sufficient to make and programme a copy that is... Let's say, *eighty per cent* accurate."

Straker considered that. "But the last twenty per cent, that's the kicker. They'll never quite be good enough. There will always be something they *can't* duplicate."

"Call it the human factor."

Straker nodded to himself. "That's what this crazy performance was about, huh? All of these mind-games and simulations, that's you trying to get into my head! Trying to get me to tell you what you don't know!"

"Absolutely right." His counterpart halted, looking back at him as they finally reached the threshold of the office block. "I want to know what you know."

He aimed the gun at the other man's head, his determination hardening. "I know *this* for certain," he said. "I'm going to finish what I started. What you've done down in the computer room... I'm going to *destroy* it."

Straker expected to encounter his ever-efficient secretary Miss Ealand as he marched his double into his outer office, but the woman was absent.

"I gave her the day off," said the Other Straker, sensing his unspoken question. "This situation would have been hard to explain, don't you think?"

"Get in there." Straker jabbed him in the shoulder with the gun barrel, and they entered the office proper. He pointed to a metal cigarette case on the desk. "You know what to do."

The other man picked up the case and flipped it open, revealing a small microphone hidden inside the lid. He offered it to his counterpart. "Care to do the honours? Unless of course you think it won't work for you?"

"*Straker*," he snapped, pitching his voice toward the device.

"*Voice identification positive: Commander Straker.*" The automated reply clicked on and the office door slid shut. A moment later, a tremor went through the floor and the entire room began to descend into the ground.

"How about that?" The other man cocked his head. "Even the machines can't tell the difference."

The manners of his twin were beginning to grate on Straker, and in a strange way, he was almost amused by the notion. *Is this how everyone else sees me*, he wondered? "You're pretty calm for a guy with a gun at his head."

"I'm just playing to type," the other man replied. "That's what's expected of me, isn't it? Ed Straker, notoriously cold-blooded and unflappable under pressure."

He bit off a terse reply as the office door reopened to reveal the corridors of the SHADO base beyond. Usually, there would have been an armed guard on duty out there, but the passageway was empty.

"Just you and me," said the Other Straker.

"Right..." He made a motion with the gun once again. "Start walking. The stairwell, on the left." He didn't want to risk being trapped in a small elevator car with his double, not now he was so close to his objective.

The other man hesitated at the top of the stairs. "All the way down?"

"All the way," Straker repeated. "Down to the depths."

They continued in silence, and Straker kept his attention focussed on the other man, even as he strained to listen for other sounds around them.

But aside from their footsteps and the ever-present hum of the base's air conditioning system, there was nothing. Even in a stand-by alert state, there should have been some indication of activity, some other sign of life. It appeared instead that the SHADO base was, like the fake streets up above, completely empty.

After a while, he couldn't hold in the question any more. "Where is everyone?"

"You gave the all-hands evacuation order," said the other man. "Or did you forget about that?"

"Still playing games with me?" He growled out the retort.

"No," came the reply. "You've got the gun. You're the one in charge, *Commander*."

They emerged on the lowermost Level E and the other man continued forward, leading him without being directed to the Computer Centre. Straker's heart thudded as his pulse began to race. Only hours ago, he had been here, darting furtively through corridors heavy with darkness, in pursuit of an enemy he couldn't catch.

But now a sense of finality was upon him. He couldn't see the shape of it yet, but the endgame for this madness was close at hand. *One way or another, this is going to finish here.*

The Other Straker halted outside the computer room, and nodded toward the long observation window that showed the interior. "This is it. The end of the line. Tell me, when you look in there, what do you see?"

He looked; and what Straker saw flooded his gut with ice. Something not of this world, something cyclopean and terrible, a great blackened mass of greenish organic matter, engulfing the central processor stack. Thick, twitching limbs like the roots of a decayed tree spread out from the core of the corruption, invading every control panel and computer bank. The air in the room was heavy with particles of corruption, spores of it caught in shafts of gelid light. And moving around in there, tending to the monstrous form like gardeners, were figures in blood-red suits and enclosed silver helmets.

"What do you see?" demanded the other man, coming closer.

Straker was still struggling to deal with the revelation that his experiences before and after chasing Jackson to the jet had been a deception. And now there was this horror laid out before him. Was it too some complex illusion, another psychological trick? Was he losing his mind?

"*Tell me what you see.*" The Other Straker was right on him, fixing him with that hard, pitiless gaze.

"Get away from me!" The violence of his visceral reaction shocked Straker into motion, and he shoved his double away, throwing himself at the door.

Straker crashed into the computer centre with a wild surge of speed, swinging around the gun in his hand. He knew what he had to do.

The aliens came at him, but Straker put them down before they could cross the distance, firing pinpoint shots that cracked through their helmet visors and sent them sprawling. Without pause, he turned the pistol on the grotesque bulk strangling SHADO's computers and unloaded every last round in the magazine, into the heart of the shrieking mass.

Empty, the pistol's slide locked open, but Straker's finger kept on pulling the trigger, click after hollow click echoing in the air.

"I did it," he breathed. "Did I do it?"

He turned to find the Other Straker standing in the open doorway, watching him with an expression that was almost regret. "Take another look. What do you see?" He asked the question one last time.

"I killed it—" Straker spun back toward the enemy he had defeated and found *nothing*. There were no alien bodies lying on the floor, no cancerous growth covering the computer banks, no spores hazing the air.

The room was exactly as it should have been, the magnetic tapes spinning and whirring as they worked, the trains of indicator lights on the panels blinking in silent sequences. Unable to grasp what he was seeing, Straker looked down at the gun in his hand, a thin wisp of cordite smoke curling from the barrel. "I don't understand."

"You didn't really think I'd let you have a deadly weapon, do you?" The other man shook his head. "Those were blank rounds. Sound and fury, signifying nothing."

"No." Straker pushed past him, back out into the corridor. "No! Those things were in there, *that's what I saw!* That's what I had to do, destroy them!"

"All through this, you kept going back to the same, driving compulsion." His counterpart's tone turned mordant. "Images in your mind, impressions of something dark and terrifying lurking down deep. Down here, on the lowest level of SHADO! In there!" He jabbed a finger at the computer room.

"Yes." The word escaped from him before he could stop it. "The enemy—"

"*You* are *the enemy!*" The Other Straker snarled at him. "You're not a man. You're not even one of *them.* You're just a tool! A self-guiding weapon, controlled by delusion and powered by fear!"

"You're lying," he gasped, his pulse hissing in his ears, his breath coming in panting chugs. "I am Edward Straker! I am commander of SHADO, this is my base, my mission, *my war!*"

"You are a copy." The other man's lip curled in a sneer. "A fake, created in some alien laboratory."

"You can't trick me," he shot back. "Not anymore! You're trying to get inside my head, find out what I know!"

Then the Other Straker's manner shifted, quieting. "One request, then. If you are Ed Straker, tell me the boy's name."

The question caught him off-guard. "Whose name?"

The other man met his gaze. "*Your son.* What is your son's name?"

Straker opened his mouth to reply, the answer forming – but there was nothing to fill the void. He looked into his recollection, seeing the face of that blond-haired young boy, his face split in a happy, infectious grin. He grasped for more, for the love he should have felt, for the memory of his only child. *And came back empty.*

"I– I remember my own son!" He shouted at his double, a crippling fear creeping into his heart. "Mary... my wife Mary, she was his mother, and his name... His name is..."

Sick with dread, he realized the awful truth. *I don't know his name. I never did.*

"You don't have that piece of information." The other man frowned. "Because *they* don't have it. They gave you everything they knew about Ed Straker, every detail they've gathered on me over the years we've been fighting this battle. But there are those gaps. That missing twenty per cent."

Straker slumped against the wall, his face filmed with sweat. His legs turned to water and he sagged, barely able to stand. *Could it be true?* The possibility was almost too much to comprehend.

"My son is dead," said the other man, a deep sorrow marbling his tone. "His name was Johnny... John Straker. I loved him as much as any father could. And he died because of me. Because of this war."

Straker searched for the echo of that same bleak pain inside himself, but it was absent. The sadness, the love, the guilt, none of that existed in him – and there could only be one reason.

"You're not the infiltrator," he said, making the truth whole as he finally gave voice to it. "*I am.*"

The two of them sat across from one another in the commander's office, mirror images of a troubled and distant man.

"There was a fire some time ago," said the Other Straker. "A random misfortune, nothing more. It happened in the records office at the hospital where Johnny died. They lost twenty years of patient's medical files in a single night, my son's among them. Everything official about my boy, turned to ash. That's why the aliens and their agents couldn't know about him. He only truly exists in here now." He tapped his chest, in the place above his heart.

"Of course," Straker replied. "That explains the... *gaps.*"

"I know this must be difficult." The other man eyed him. "I'd offer you a stiff drink, but—"

"But *I*... I mean *we* don't touch the stuff." He leaned forward and took a cigar. "This will have to do." The other man followed suit, and offered him a light. He took a draw and exhaled, struggling to make sense of everything. "You took a very big risk, with me. Why all this subterfuge?"

"Why not just terminate you and be done with it, you mean?" The Other Straker frowned. "I won't lie, the thought did cross my mind. Quite frankly, that's exactly what Paul Foster advocated for from the very start. And Doctor Frazer, well... he was very interested in opening you up to see what makes you tick."

"That's why Foster was so insubordinate when I was giving orders, huh?" He shook his head. It also explained away the coldly calculating manner Frazer had shown in his interactions over the past few days.

"I wanted to know what you were made of," said the other man. "To find out how much of me was in you."

"Did everyone know? Jackson had to be a part of it."

He nodded. "He was. He embraced the idea more than anyone, saw it as a unique opportunity to gain intelligence. Jackson handled the programmes of hypnotic suggestion and the psychotropics. But Alec wasn't in the loop, at least not at first. You see, if I had to put a line on it, I would say there's no man on earth who knows Ed Straker better than Alec Freeman."

"You didn't tell him because you wanted to see how he would react."

He nodded again. "If you could fool Alec... you could fool anyone."

"And did I?"

The Other Straker exhaled a breath of cigar smoke. "You came close, I'll give you that."

He swallowed hard. "I didn't know..."

"And that's why it almost worked. The best spy is the one who's never aware that's what they are. But you couldn't be allowed to succeed. The aliens implanted that fear compulsion in you, driving you to the computer centre. If you'd followed it through to a logical conclusion, you would have destroyed every system in that room. The result? Total chaos throughout SHADO."

"I thought I was doing my duty..." His throat went dry. "But it would have left the planet wide open to attack."

"It's exactly the kind of ploy we've come to expect from our enemy. Elaborate and insidious." The other man paused, framing his words. "But they failed because they don't understand us. The aliens believed they know Ed Straker, because they have the hard facts of who he is." He gave a rueful smile. "I know what people say about me; *Commander Straker's a cold fish. Ruthless. Clinical. Dogged.* All those things are true, after a fashion. But that's not the sum of who I am. No matter how much of a man you can read... you still can't see into his soul."

Straker stared into the middle distance. "So how did I... get here? I remember a road, at night, then waking up in the Medical Section. Is that your memory or is it mine?"

"Jackson's ESP tester is real," said the other man. "But that story about it putting you into a coma was the cover. We needed a plausible excuse for the missing time that you... that *I* would be willing to accept."

"But to replace a senior SHADO officer, the aliens would have to neutralize the original." He thought it through, wincing as jolts of pain stabbed at his skull. It was as if his own mind was trying to stop him thinking about it. "Capture you... or kill you."

"We think that was the plan. A u-foe made it through our defences, and they had to sacrifice two other ships to do it. It landed in a field in Southern England. On board was an alien assassin... and a single infiltrator."

Straker remembered the grass beneath his feet as he sleep-walked toward a five-barred gate, and the vague impression of someone in red and silver at his side. The sun had just set and it was twilight. Emerald light pulsed behind him, throbbing like a heartbeat. "But you were already there."

"Yes. A lucky turn of events, a Mobile that happened to be in the right place at the right time. Foster was leading the ground force, and when the u-foe tried to take off, it was blown out of the air. The alien died in the firefight that followed, but we got a live prisoner."

"Me." At the edges of his recollection, barred by more jagged jolts of pain, Straker could just about grasp the sense-memory of something burning, of hissing gunshots in the darkness, and a terrible sense of disruption.

"I have to say, it was unnerving when Foster brought you in," said the Other Straker. "But the situation represented a unique opportunity. So we turned our enemy's plan in on itself."

Straker nodded slowly. "It's what I would have done." That peculiar sort of calm spread through him once more, and the pain in his head finally receded, washing out like a retreating tide. Acceptance, so it seemed, brought with it some small measure of peace.

Discarding the cigar, he reached forward over the desk and picked up a framed photograph, tucked out of the way in one corner where it was easy to miss. The picture was the same one Jackson had shown him during his tests, of Straker's wife Mary and his son John together in better days. His fingers touched the image and he felt a profound sense of loss.

"I don't usually put that out on display," said the other man. "It can be... a distraction. But today I wanted to look at it again."

"I feel like I know them, but I don't. It's an illusion. It's your life, not mine."

"I'm sorry." The Other Straker's remorse was genuine.

He handed back the photo and met the other man's gaze. "What happens now?"

"Now...." His counterpart looked down at the picture. "We end this."

CHAPTER SIX

RESOLUTIONS

The Kingfisher's twin ducted rotors thrummed as the VTOL aircraft raced through the morning at tree-top level. Foster kept it fast and low, guiding them over the shallow rises of hills and down along the line of river valleys.

In the co-pilot's seat, Foster's commanding officer spoke into his headset. "Status of the target?"

"*Unchanged.*" Keith Ford's voice came back immediately, the lieutenant broadcasting from the controller's station at SHADO headquarters. "*Sightings from Moonbase and SID remain consistent with positive track.*"

"If any deviation occurs, no matter how small, I want to know about it the second it happens, clear?"

"*Clear, sir.*"

"Straker out." He turned toward Foster. "Keep the rotors idling when you put us down, Paul. If this goes wrong, we may need to get out of here in a hurry."

"Understood." Foster made no attempt to hide his irritation at this entire exercise.

"Got something to add, Colonel?" The other man caught on immediately. "Come on, spit it out."

"With all due respect, Commander," he replied. "You know there's a much simpler way to send the aliens a message. One with no equivocation." Foster thought about the pistol holstered on his belt. "I can imagine it might be difficult for you to do... I could handle it."

"Finish things with a single bullet, huh?"

"I doubt they'd give one of us any better consideration."

"We are not *them*, Foster. And frankly, I find your eagerness to terminate my doppelganger to be slightly disturbing."

He frowned, guiding the Kingfisher toward its designated landing site in the fallow field up ahead. "Doesn't it give you the creeps? I can't look at it without my skin crawling."

"I'm not sure if I should be insulted by that." The other man leaned in. "He's a *person*, not an *it*. Maybe not like you and me, but still a living being."

Foster slowed the aircraft to a hover and flipped a lever to extend the Kingfisher's undercarriage. He brought it down to the ground with a gentle bump, the downwash from the rotors blowing away a torrent of grass and fallen leaves.

Glancing around, he saw nothing but empty meadows and distant stands of trees in all directions. SHADO had made certain there was no-one around for miles, but had it been his call to make, Foster would have concealed a force of mortar-firing Mobiles within firing range.

He asked the question that had been preying on his mind from the very start. "You ever think you're too close to this?"

"That's why you're here." Straker studied him carefully. "To watch my back."

Foster brought the engines to idle, then fixed his commander with a hard look. "We don't owe *him* anything. There's no Geneva Convention for prisoners of war with extra-terrestrial origins. Give Frazer and Jackson what they want, and we might still be able to salvage something of value from all this."

Straker sighed. "How do you think this war is going to end, Paul?"

"We beat them." Foster snorted. "We push them back at every turn. Shoot down every u-foe, stymie every scheme they cook up, for as long as it takes. We keep going until they're gone."

"And if we can't? What if this fight drags on, and on, and on? Do we bequeath it to the next generation? Some endless cold war, grinding away in secret until one side makes the mistake that ends it for everyone?"

"What's the alternative? Sue for peace?" He shook his head. "You've said it yourself, Commander. The aliens are predators, and they treat us like prey animals. And last time I looked, I didn't see any lions making friends with the zebras."

Straker looked at his wristwatch, then peered up out of the canopy, into the clear blue sky above. "Not long now." He took a breath, then turned back to Foster. "I don't disagree with you. But we don't have the luxury of looking at this conflict from only one angle, down the barrel of a gun. I am the commander of SHADO, and my job is to stop the aliens, by whatever means necessary. So there is no option I will not explore, no opportunity I will not take, until that mission is accomplished. Do you understand?"

"I do," allowed Foster. "But I don't have to like it."

Straker unstrapped from his seat. "I'm going back into the cargo bay. You let me know the moment you get a visual sighting."

"Yes sir." Foster put a hand on his arm and Straker paused. "And just in case?" He drew his weapon and offered it up.

Straker shook his head and pushed past him.

The Kingfisher's rear bay was a cramped space, with barely enough room for the two of them.

Straker's duplicate sat on a seat folded out of the bulkhead, a hollow thousand-yard stare in his gaze. "Where have you brought me?"

"Back to where it began," he replied, indicating the exterior hatch.

"What's out there? What's the point of this?"

"I'm sending you back," said Straker. "That u-foe hiding out beyond lunar orbit, the one SID was tracking? They were there to watch over you. Waiting to see if you succeeded in your mission."

"And now they're coming here?"

He gave a nod. "Moonbase is tracking their approach as we speak. I've ordered the Interceptors to let the ship cross our lines unmolested. Sky One will observe from a distance as they pass through the atmosphere, but will not engage. They've got a free pass, all the way here."

"They know that I failed." The other man shook his head. "Somehow, they know."

"Commander?" Foster called out from the cockpit. "Just got word from Captain Waterman. He's tailing the u-foe, it's sixty seconds out, closing fast."

"Let's go." Straker opened the hatch, and followed his counterpart out into the daylight.

The two men walked away from the Kingfisher, and high up in the sky, sunshine flashed off spinning discs of silver. In the distance, over the low thrum of the idling tilt-rotors, Straker picked out the glassy sound of a rising-falling cadence.

"I want you to do something for me," he told the other man. "I want you to give them a message. Tell them: as long as they keep coming, we will keep fighting. To the last man on Earth, if needs be. We know their tricks. We're always watching. And we will not surrender."

"They know," his duplicate said again, as the rushing noise of the UFO's approach grew louder.

Straker looked up as the alien vessel crested the trees at speed before coming to a sudden, physics-defying stop in mid-air. He could feel the waves of controlled gravitation warping the atmosphere around it, and he backed away. The hissing whirr of the vessel shifted in pitch as it came down on to the grass, the green glow of strange energies spilling over its metallic structure.

He'd rarely been this close to one of the alien machines. Straker took it in, the analytical part of his mind filing his impressions away for later review, in case some small observation might give another clue to the nature of his enemy – and how, ultimately, to defeat them.

His counterpart took a step toward the craft, then halted, looking back. "What's going to happen to me? What am I supposed to do?" There was a plaintive quality to the questions.

"*Survive*," said Straker. "That's the only thing I know for certain we have in common. The will to live."

The other man approached the UFO, and a hatch opened like an iris, the silver skin of the craft parting seamlessly. He stepped through, and it closed behind him, the metal sealing as if the entrance had never been there.

Immediately, the tempo of the alien vessel's power field changed and it began to spin again around its central axis. Lifting off the ground, its speed increased and it held its hover for a long second.

Straker braced himself. *If they want me dead, this is the perfect opportunity.* A single lightning-like flash from the UFO's energy weapon could reduce him to atoms, along with Foster and the Kingfisher.

But then the craft shot skyward in a perfect ballistic trajectory, straight up toward the cloudless blue. He heard the double-thud of a sonic boom, watching it diminish into a flickering silver dot, then disappear.

At length, Straker climbed back into the Kingfisher's cockpit, to find Foster with one hand pressed to his headset. "Sky One couldn't keep up, it went straight to escape velocity," he reported. "But SID has a positive track. There's still time to deploy the Interceptors. You only have to give the word."

He shook his head. "Let him go."

Alec Freeman crossed the command centre with swift strides, nodding to the operators who looked up to catch his eye – Keith Ford, at the controller's post, Ayshea Johnson at the tracker's station – and did his best to project a reassuring air of quiet confidence to his subordinates.

It had been an odd few days at SHADO, and that was saying something. The work of tracking, logging and watching the skies went on around the clock, and it could almost become commonplace if you let it. Sometimes it was important to remember exactly how *uncommon* their work really was, and of what was at stake. Freeman tapped the file folders in his hand against his side as he walked, moving on to the commander's office as the silver door hummed open to grant him entry.

Paul Foster was waiting inside, leaning against the edge of the conference table, a cup of coffee in his hand. He saluted Freeman with it. "Alec."

"Paul." Freeman made a show of looking around. "Are we both early, or is the boss late?"

"The former. He's always on time, you know that."

"True."

Foster pointed at the files. "Is that Jackson's report?"

"And mine too." He nodded, dropping the paperwork on to Straker's desk, atop Foster's own file already waiting for the commander's approval. "I've skimmed the high points of the good doctor's recommendations," he went on. "It doesn't bode well. This latest incident means we're going to have to activate a whole new tier of security checks and reviews, and roll them out across the entire organization. Everyone in SHADO will have to be re-evaluated, from top to bottom."

"Lovely. I can't wait." Foster grimaced at the thought. "But it's got to be done. We can't ignore the risk, not after..." He trailed off.

Freeman crossed the room, examining the slowly-moving Earth-Moon model in the alcove. "He convinced me, you know. At least, at first. I really believed I was talking to Ed Straker."

"You were, in a manner of speaking," said Foster. "That's what makes it so disturbing."

"I'd love to lie through my teeth and say, *oh, I knew the moment I clapped eyes on him he was a fake*... but no." He considered that for a moment. "I think I did sense something was off, but not so much it rang the alarm bells. It's enough to make a man doubt his perceptions."

Foster nodded. "Sometimes instinct is all we have to go on. It's just hard to make that look convincing when you're writing up the account after the fact."

Freeman made a grunt of agreement. "You know, even though their plan to lobotomise SHADO failed, the aliens have still got one over on us. Now we're going to have to dedicate time, money and resources to those new security measures, and that'll take focus off the main job."

"And every penny spent on double-checking our own people is a penny less toward keeping our birds in the air." Foster covered the sour comment with a sip of coffee. "I take it the u-foe carrying the other guy is gone?"

"Long gone," Freeman confirmed. "Is it strange I feel sorry for him? I don't get the sense the aliens are tolerant of mistakes."

Foster's lip curled in a brief, humourless smile. "Are we sure we got the right one back? I have to wonder..."

The other man let that comment hang, and after a moment Freeman continued. "You think Straker made a bad choice." It wasn't a question.

"It's not my place to say."

"But you're going to anyway."

Foster put the coffee aside and fixed Freeman with a hard look. "Do you ever think that maybe we're doing this the wrong way? Fighting a defensive conflict, time and time again?" He gestured at the space model. "Perhaps we should take things to them. Let the aliens know what it's like to be the invaded, not the invaders."

"And how would we get there? NASA, the Russians, EUROSEC, nobody has any rockets that could make the trip. And those nuclear-powered designs the World Space Commission are building won't be ready for years." Freeman sighed. "I share your frustration, Paul, I really do. But we have to face the battle in front of us, not the one we want to fight."

Foster took a step closer, his voice dropping. "How long can we keep this up, Alec? I know you've asked yourself the same question. SHADO's secrets won't stay hidden forever. There are people out there who want to go back to the Moon, civilians and scientists who want to build space probes and orbital stations... we can't keep them grounded forever."

"There are ways of discouraging that," said Freeman. "We make sure political leaders stay focussed on earthbound issues."

"But how far does it go?" Foster pressed. "Is there a group of SHADO agents out there, quietly sabotaging rocket launches and erasing evidence of u-foe sightings?"

"I don't know." Freeman blew out a breath and shook his head. "It's above my pay-grade."

"One day, something's going to happen that we can't cover up," Foster said darkly, as the office door slid open. "And we'd better be ready."

Straker entered the room and marched toward the two men, and it was clear that he'd heard those last few words. "You might be right, Colonel," he said firmly, "but that day isn't today." He turned to his desk and picked up the reports, briskly thumbing through them. "This is everything?"

"It's all there," Foster confirmed, exchanging a look with Freeman.

Freeman spoke again, in a guarded tone. "Ed, if we need to discuss the fallout from this—"

Straker's terse response cut him off before he could finish. "There's nothing to debate. We move forward. We continue the mission." He took his seat, still scanning the contents of the files. "Colonel Freeman will return to the secondary base construction site and relieve Colonel Lake, I want her back here as soon as possible. Colonel Foster, I want you to liaise with Lieutenant Ellis, get me a complete status update on Moonbase operations by the end of the day." When neither man moved immediately, Straker looked up and his eyes narrowed. "Get to it!" he ordered.

As the two of them left the office, Foster made a last comment out of the side of his mouth to Freeman: "I guess we did get the right one after all."

The door thudded shut, leaving Straker alone. He let the reports drop on his desk and reached for one of the telephone handsets. As he did so, his fingers passed over the small picture frame still resting there, and he hesitated.

He picked up the photograph and allowed himself a moment to step outside the man that he had to be, every hour of every day. He lost himself in Mary's beautiful eyes, in his son's bright smile. He reached for the warm memory of them, cupping it in his hands as if it were a tiny candle flame to be protected from the wind.

Then the picture frame went into a desk drawer and stayed there, and Commander Edward Straker returned to the matter at hand; to the mission.

ACKNOWLEDGMENTS

The author would like to thank the cast and crew of *UFO* for creating the unique and enduring telefantasy adventure series this novella is based upon. Much appreciation must also go to Chris Bentley, author of *The Complete Book of Gerry Anderson's UFO* and to Chris Thompson and Andrew Clements, co-authors of the *UFO S.H.A.D.O. Technical Operations Manual*, for their sterling works of reference which provided an authoritative foundation for this story. In addition, many thanks to Jamie Anderson and Nicholas Briggs for extending the invitation to tell a tale in this shadowy world of aliens and unknowns – and finally, a heartfelt salute to Gerry Anderson, whose adventure stories shaped a generation.

OTHER GREAT TITLES
BY ANDERSON
ENTERTAINMENT

available from
shop.gerryanderson.com

Five Star Five: John Lovell and the Zargon Threat

THE TIME: THE FUTURE
THE PLACE: THE UNIVERSE

The peaceful planet of Kestra is under threat. The evil Zargon forces are preparing to launch a devastating attack from an asteroid fortress. With the whole Kestran system in the Zargons' sights, Colonel Zana looks to one man to save them. Except one man isn't enough.

Gathering a crack team around him including a talking chimpanzee, a marauding robot and a mystic monk, John Lovell must infiltrate the enemy base and save Kestra from the Zargons!

Five Star Five: The Doomsday Device

THE TIME: THE FUTURE
THE PLACE: THE UNIVERSE

The Zargon home world is dying. With their nemesis in prison on trumped up charges, they have developed a brand-new weapon of awesome power.

As the Zargons plot another attempt on the planet Kestra, a group of friends must band together and rescue their only hope for survival – John Lovell!

Five Star Five: The Battle for Kestra

THE TIME: THE FUTURE
THE PLACE: THE UNIVERSE

As the Zargons prepare their last, desperate attempt to invade their enemy planet, John Lovell and his gang of misfits stand accused of acts of terror on Kestran soil.

With a new President in place, the 'Five Star Five' are forced underground before they can confront the enemy within and thwart the Zargons' plans.

Intergalactic Rescue 4: Stellar Patrol

It is the 22nd century. The League of Planets has tasked Jason Stone, Anne Warran and their two robots, Alpha and Zeta to explore the galaxy, bringing hope to those in need of rescue.

On board Intergalactic Rescue 4, they travel to ice moons and jungle planets in ten exciting adventures that see them journey further across the stars than anyone before.

But what are the secret transmissions that Anne discovers?

And why do their rescues seem to be taking them on a predetermined course?

Soon, Anne discovers that her co-pilot, Jason, might be on a quest of his own...

A GERRY ANDERSON PRODUCTION

Thunderbirds: Terror from the Stars

Thunderbird Five is attacked by an unknown enemy with uncanny powers. An unidentified object is tracked landing in the Gobi desert, but what's the connection? Scott Tracy races to the scene in the incredible Thunderbird One, but he cannot begin to imagine the terrible danger he is about to encounter.

Alone in the barren wilderness, he is possessed by a malevolent intelligence and assigned a fiendish mission – one which, if successful, will have the most terrifying consequences for the entire world.

International Rescue are about to face their most astounding adventure yet!

Thunderbirds: Peril in Peru

An early warning of disaster brings International Rescue to Peru to assist in relief efforts following a series of earth tremors – and sends the Thunderbirds in search of an ancient Inca treasure trove hidden beneath a long-lost temple deep in the South American jungle!

When Lady Penelope is kidnapped by sinister treasure hunters, Scott Tracy and Parker are soon hot on their trail.

Along the way they'll have to solve a centuries-old mystery, brave the inhospitable wilderness of the jungle and even tangle with a lost tribe – with the evil Hood close behind them all the way…

Thunderbirds: Operation Asteroids

What starts out as a simple rescue mission to save a trapped miner on the Moon, soon turns out to be one of International Rescue's greatest catastrophes. After the Hood takes members of International Rescue hostage during the rescue, a chase across space and an altercation among the asteroids only worsens the situation.

With the Hood hijacking Thunderbird Three along with Brains, Lady Penelope and Tin-Tin, it is up to the Tracy brothers to stage a daring rescue in the mountain tops of his hidden lair.

But can they rescue Brains before his engineering genius is used for the destructive forces of evil?

STINGRAY

Stingray: Operation Icecap

The Stingray crew discover an ancient diving bell that leads them on an expeditionary voyage through the freezing waters of Antarctica to the land of a lost civilisation.

Close on the heels of Troy Tempest and the pride of the World Aquanaut Security Patrol is the evil undersea ruler Titan. Ahead of them are strange creatures who inhabit underground waterways and an otherworldly force with hidden powers strong enough to overwhelm even Stingray's defences.

Stingray: Monster from the Deep

Commander Shore's old enemy, Conrad Hagen, is out of prison and back on the loose with his beautiful but devious daughter, Helga. When they hijack a World Aquanaut Security Patrol vessel and kidnap Atlanta, it's up to Captain Troy Tempest and the crew of Stingray to save her.

But first they will have to uncover the mystery of the treasure of Sanito Cathedral and escape the fury of the monster from the deep.

SPACE: 1999 Maybe There –
The Lost Stories from SPACE: 1999

Strap into your Moon Ship and prepare for a trip to an alternate universe!

Gathered here for the first time are the original stories written in the early days of production on the internationally acclaimed television series SPACE: 1999. Uncover the differences between Gerry and Sylvia Anderson's original story Zero G, George Bellak's first draft of The Void Ahead and Christopher Penfold's uncredited shooting script Turning Point. Each of these tales shows the evolution of the pilot episode with scenes and characters that never made it to the screen.

Wonder at a tale that was NEVER filmed where the Alpha People, desperate to migrate to a new home, instigate a conflict between two alien races. Also included are Christopher Penfold's original storylines for Guardian of Piri and Dragon's Domain, an adaption of Keith Miles's early draft for All That Glisters and read how Art Wallace (Dark Shadows) originally envisioned the episode that became Matter of Life and Death.

Discover how SPACE: 1999 might have been had they gone 'Maybe There?'

The Armageddon Engine

Adrift in deep space, Commander John Koenig and the people of Moonbase Alpha face an uncertain fate when a planet-killing alien weapon at the heart of a sinister cloud diverts their lost Moon on to a fatal trajectory.

As each moment brings the Moon closer to total obliteration, Koenig leads a desperate mission into the unknown to save all life on Alpha. Does hope lie among a rag-tag colony of refugees hiding in the shadow of devastation? Or can the Alphans find a path into the heart of the war machine and end its destructive rampage? With time running out, the answer will mean the difference between survival... or annihilation.

Damaged Goods

First Action Bureau exists to protect the Earth from criminal elements before they get the chance to act. Using decades of 'big data' and globally connected quantum artificial intelligence, First Action Bureau is able to predict criminal activity before it occurs...

Nero Jones has led a troubled life, but things are about to get a whole lot worse... Press-ganged into joining First Action Bureau, a shadowy organisation set up to counter terrorist threats, Nero finds herself thrown into a range of increasingly more exciting missions under the guidance of the mysterious Nathan Drake.

As she learns more about the Bureau, she's haunted by half-forgotten memories that lead her to question everything she knows. Just what is real and what is fake? As she delves deeper into the Bureau's history, she comes to a startling conclusion; nothing is true!